MW00577443

CIRQUE

DES

MASQUES

USA TODAY & WALL STREET JOURNAL BESTSELLING AUTHOR

BECCA STEELE

Cirque des Masques

Copyright © 2023 by Becca Steele

Editing by Rumi

Cover by TRC Designs

Becca Steele

www.authorbeccasteele.com

AUTHOR'S NOTE

The author is British, and this story contains British English spellings and phrases.

Please note that this book may contain triggers for some readers. Please view the trigger warnings page below for details:
https://authorbeccasteele.com/trigger-warnings/

For anyone who wanted to run away and join the circus, as I once did...
Although this particular circus wasn't quite what I had in mind...

I, myself, am strange and unusual.

— TIM BURTON, *BEETLEJUICE*

THE LEGEND OF THE SHOW...

They called it the Cirque des Masques. *The Circus of Masks.* Legend said that it had been founded in France, with the circus journeying into Eastern Europe during the Middle Ages when the English were waging war against the French. One thing led to another, the circus changing hands over the years, the reasons lost in the mists of time. Ownership fell first to the Russians, then to the Germans for a brief period, followed by the Romanians. Eventually, in 1742, the circus found its home in the British Isles, occasionally criss-crossing into northern France, constantly on the move, never staying in one place for long.

Rumours followed the circus wherever it went. Tales of shadows, of darkness, of people disappearing without explanation. Those who were less inclined to believe such fantasies simply remarked that the myths were perpetrated by the owners of the circus themselves in order to cultivate an air of mystery, to create a sense of adventure that would have patrons flocking in their droves for a chance to claim one of the coveted tickets.

Then there were the performers. Always clad in black with shades of red, the bright scarlet of freshly spilt blood.

Always masked.

It was said that those who caught a glimpse of the person behind the mask would be cursed for all eternity.

Was there any truth to the rumours?

Let us find out...

I

DIMA

lood pooled on the dirty ground, making my cock lengthen against my will. So warm. So thick and delicious. So...full of life.

I *wanted*. I *craved*. I needed a release.

It was a sickness. A disease. Pure bloodlust filling my senses, taking over what was left of my connection to humanity.

It was the same for us all. They said that the circus performers cursed others, yet we were the ones who were cursed. We were bound together by our unnatural cravings, unable to live a normal life, always on the move, always running, and never looking back.

In the centre of the circle at my feet, Florin cradled the woman in his arms. His blade glittered in the flickering candlelight as he gracefully sliced across her throat, crimson spraying in a delicate arc. We stood there in silence, watching until her screams stopped and her struggles slowed to nothing. As her body paled and her life drained away, he lowered her to the floor, gently closing her eyes, and placed a kiss on the place he had sliced her open. When he raised his head, I saw the streaks of scarlet dripping down his face.

My cock hardened further. Another side effect of my bloodlust, and it was nothing to do with the woman. Death didn't turn me on—not at all. No, it was the sight of the pearls of red that ran down Florin's beautiful face, trailing down his throat and into the collar of his shirt. With his perfectly sculpted, lithe body, an abundance of blond curls, and huge blue eyes, he was angelic-looking. But looks could be deceiving. He was the most vicious of the members of our small, tight-knit group. A killer who *enjoyed* killing.

"Fuck, why do I always get hard watching Florin act like a psycho?" Darius muttered from next to me, shaking his head. He was cursed with the high sex drive that was another hallmark of our kind.

Neither craving could ever fully be satisfied, to my knowledge.

Normal people had it so easy, going about their lives blissfully unaware. They'd never know what it was like to burn from the inside, to be driven insane with need... to become so delirious with that need that for some, hallucinations would begin. To be so driven out of one's mind with both bloodlust and sexual yearning, one would do things that would never, ever be acceptable if one were in their right mind.

We were all tainted, *wrong*. There was no redemption in our futures, so all we could do was continue this never-ending cycle until inevitably, we would be replaced. And the cycle would begin all over again.

"Darius," I gritted out. "We need..."

His gaze shot to mine, the pupils of his midnight eyes blown wide and blacker than black. "*Ey*, Dima. Kristoff and Tanner are on call. We will go now."

Within a few minutes, we were seated inside the back of the blacked-out Range Rover, Kristoff eyeing us warily in the rear-view mirror as he steered the SUV towards the nearest club in whatever town we were due to perform in. He worried about us, as did all the members of the small, rotating team that we employed as security. They were the best of the best, covering our tracks and allowing us to move from place to place like shadows in the night, leaving nothing but memories behind. All of us were orphans, and other than the ringmaster, they were the closest we had to parental figures in our own fucked-up, twisted family.

The tang of citrus filled the car's interior, and both Darius and I took deep breaths, the fresh scent helping to clear both our lungs and our heads, giving us a temporary respite, and allowing us to think more clearly.

"We're here," Kristoff announced unnecessarily as he pulled to a stop outside the club's entrance. I glanced at myself in the rear-view mirror, satisfied with my appearance. I was lucky enough to inherit my black hair, smooth, pale skin, and piercing blue eyes from whomever had a hand in my DNA. Many were struck by my beauty, both men and women, and that was a bonus when one suffered from the affliction of an extremely high sex drive.

"See you later," Darius murmured, sliding out of the car. I did a double take when I noticed the psycho boy himself, Florin, leaning casually against the wall next to the entrance, sliding his fingers over a shining silver knife with a rather manic smile on his face. As I watched, Darius strode over to Florin, and Florin tipped up his chin. Then Darius was lowering his head to capture Florin's lips, and I held my breath, half expecting that wickedly sharp-looking knife to impale my friend.

Except it didn't, and as I watched, Darius yanked Florin into him and then their hands and mouths were all over each other.

Fuck.

My cock was harder than ever. I threw open the SUV's door, stumbling outside and making a beeline for the club's entrance. The doorman said something, but I paid him no attention, adjusting the lapels of my fitted black suit as I strode inside.

Reaching the VIP section, I was waved in by the bouncer. Kristoff or Tanner would have called ahead to ensure privacy—out there in the main part of the club it was too dangerous. Too many variables. The VIP section was less crowded, with a more discerning clientele.

My gaze swept across the space.

And stopped.

A slow smile curved over my lips.

Yes. He would do nicely.

Very, very nicely indeed.

2

OLLIE

The drinks were flowing, and it was all I could do to keep up with the orders.

I probably shouldn't have been here, but Jai was sick and I'd promised to cover his shift. I normally worked on the main floor while my friend took care of this part of the club, but I couldn't say no to the extra money.

After all, I needed it. My rent was due at the beginning of next week and as a more-or-less illegal tenant in a sublet, I wasn't in any position to bargain. I had to pay up on time, or else I'd be out on the streets. Again.

Being a nineteen-year-old with zero prospects should've been depressing, but I'd learned to make my peace with it. I had no family, but my housemates were alright, and my work colleagues had taken me under their wing from the first day.

I mixed what felt like my hundredth mojito, my body

so used to it that I was able to switch my brain off entirely. Idly scanning the VIP area while I strained the mixture into a glass, I found myself smiling. I liked this job. I liked the fact that I knew exactly what to do here. Knew what the patrons expected of me. Maybe some people would look down on my current profession, but I didn't care, because I was *good* at this.

My idle thoughts screeched to a halt the second I met a piercing blue gaze all the way over on the other side of the VIP area. A man was sitting there, casually reclining against the plush leather booth. He was every single one of my fantasies come to life. Blacker-than-black hair, smooth skin that held the hint of a tan, and full, red lips, and even from here, I could see how those azure eyes were framed by long, coal black lashes. And his body...the black suit he was wearing lovingly caressed every muscle, every curve, showcasing his hard, uncompromising lines.

Fucking fuck. This man looked rich and expensive, and way, way out of my league. Like some kind of dark mafia prince, like someone I would bow down to if I was given the chance.

I drank him in. And then I looked closer.

The expression on his face...it gave me dark, dangerous vibes. It was something indescribable. Something that set me on edge.

"Oi, Ollie! Get your head out of your ass and finish up the order, would ya?"

A loud voice brought me out of my daze, and I

suddenly realised that I'd been standing there, frozen in place with the empty cocktail shaker in my hand.

"Sorry," I muttered to Pen, who was my supervisor and current fellow bartender. She rolled her eyes, discreetly pointing towards the group of glasses that made up my half-finished order. I wasted no time filling the rest of the glasses, collapsing against the back of the bar with a relieved sigh when I was done.

While there was a short lull in the mixing action, I grabbed a soft cloth and began wiping down the bar surface. I'd just reached the end of the bar when a hand closed over mine.

A shock of electricity raced up my arm, making my hairs stand on end. It was only my instincts, honed from my years growing up in less-than-desirable circumstances, that kept me from outwardly reacting. *Never show your hand.*

Except, when I lifted my head and met those intense blue eyes, I knew I couldn't stop my own eyes from widening.

His nostrils flared as he stared down at me with his mesmerising gaze. It was probably my wild imagination, but it seemed as if he was almost brimming with raw, magnetic power. It was hypnotic.

From farther down the bar came the sound of clattering glasses, and the spell was broken.

I stepped back, withdrawing my hand from beneath his. His jaw tightened, but he remained silent.

"What can I get you, sir?" I put on my best customer

service voice, pretending to myself that I wasn't fazed by the sheer beauty of this man.

He hummed, sliding his gaze from mine to scan the rows of bottles behind the bar. When he spoke, his voice was a low, smooth purr that made my breath catch in my throat. "I'm afraid that what I want isn't on the menu."

I tried to remember what Jai had told me about the VIP section. "We have other options that aren't listed. What are you looking for?"

"I've already found what I'm looking for." A slow, sinful smile curved over his lips. "I'd say he's...hmmm... maybe five-foot-seven or eight...with golden brown waves and sweet honey eyes...and a pretty mouth that I'd like to see wrapped around my cock. Do you know anyone who would fit that description?"

For the first time in my life, I was completely speechless. This man was interested in *me*? I internally shook my head. *Don't be a fucking idiot, Ol.* He was obviously playing with me, thinking it was amusing to make me flustered.

"What would you like to drink, Mr....?"

"Call me Dima." The name was immediately followed by a muttered curse, his eyes widening for a second. He recovered his composure so quickly that I wondered if I'd imagined that brief look of shock that had flared in his gaze. "Now I'm at a disadvantage. You'll have to even the odds."

"Ollie," I said. There was no point in giving a fake name, not here where my real name was used by the other members of staff. "Or Oliver, if you want to be formal." My mouth twisted for a second and he laughed.

"Ollie. When do you next get a break?" Pulling the sleeve of his jacket up, he glanced at a chunky silver wristwatch and then back to me.

Was he seriously suggesting... "Why?"

One brow raised, and he swiped his tongue across his lips, his mouth curving into a smirk as he observed me tracking the movement. "Because I want you to suck my cock. I thought I made that obvious?"

I stared at him in disbelief. "What if I'm not into men? You can't just assume—"

"Oh, sweetheart, you're much easier to read than you think. I saw the way you were eye-fucking me earlier. You want me, so let's not waste any time here. I don't have long, and I'd like you to be the one to suck my cock. Are you interested, or should I find someone else?"

Who *was* this guy?

He was still smirking, so I glared at him, even though we both knew I wasn't fooling anyone. "Fine." I folded my arms across my chest. I glanced over at Pen, mouthing, *Break*? She nodded, holding up her fingers to indicate I had ten minutes. "I can take a quick break now, I guess."

Instead of a reply, he just raised his brows, giving me an expectant look. The way he was acting should probably have been a turn-off, but who was I kidding? This guy was hands down the hottest man I'd ever seen, and if he wanted me to be the one to suck him off, who was I to argue? Chances like this didn't come around... ever. Not for someone like me.

I stepped out from behind the bar and right up to his chest, tilting my head to meet his gaze. He looked down at me, still far too amused.

My first instinct was to scowl at him, but now that it seemed like this was really happening, I didn't want him to change his mind. "Where do you want to do this? You don't look like the type to go at it in a dirty alley."

A dark chuckle fell from his mouth. "Oh, you'd be surprised at the places I've fucked, sweet boy."

Boy? I wasn't a fucking boy, and I had the birth certificate to prove it. Okay, I didn't actually have a copy anymore. It had been lost somewhere over the years. Moving from place to place meant that it was easy to lose track of possessions. But I knew that my date of birth was correct because it had been confirmed enough times. The police had my records, including my fingerprints. You shoplift once or twice...oh, and get caught passing on some less-than-legal merch, and you're branded a criminal when all you're trying to do is get by in life.

"I'm not a fucking boy," I growled, and he chuckled again, amused.

"Relax, sweetheart." His gaze raked over me, and he licked his lips. "It's just an expression. I can see that you're all man. Now, are you going to show me this alleyway? Time's ticking."

Dropping my insincere attempts at a protest, because they were a waste of both my time and his, I headed over to the locked door that led into the alleyway. Not the hook-up alley, but the one that the staff used. It led to a small parking area with a group of large, industrial bins. It would be quieter here, with much less risk of being seen. As much as I did want to give this sexy stranger a blowjob, I'd rather not have one of the patrons recognise me. I could kiss my job goodbye if I was found out, and I needed the money.

We'd just drawn level with the first bin when he yanked me into him, hard, his hand wrapping around my throat as he pulled me into the shadows, his breath shockingly hot in my ear after the chill of the winter night breeze.

"This will do."

I couldn't reply because *he'd cut off my circulation.* Throwing my elbow back, I aimed for his solar plexus, but he laughed, easily dodging the blow, and twisted us around so that I was pinned against the wall with his hard body pressed all up against mine.

Including his cock. His very large cock, if what I was feeling was anything to go by. My own cock was like an iron bar, straining against the front of my trousers...as it had been since his hand had landed on top of mine across the bar, if I was going to be truthful with myself.

Letting my head fall back against the cold stone, I stared up at him, swiping my tongue across my lips. I really wanted him to kiss me, to know how that gorgeous mouth would taste against mine. Kissing wasn't something I'd ever had much experience with...or at least not kissing for pleasure.

"Sorry. I don't do kisses." It almost sounded like the

regret in his tone was real as he bypassed my waiting mouth, his lips travelling down my throat. His large hand slid down my chest to where my erection was pressing against the seam of my trousers.

I moaned, arching into his grip as he rubbed my bulge.

"Fucking delicious," he murmured, his teeth clamping down on my throat almost hard enough to break the skin, and the pleasure-pain combination was fucking euphoric. "You like that, hmm? Want more?" Licking across the place he'd just bitten, he eased my trousers open.

"Yes. Fuck. Please." I finally dared to touch him, sliding my arms around his waist so I could get my hands on his tight, muscular ass.

"After." Withdrawing his hand from my trousers, he took a step back. "First, you need to give me what you promised."

I fell to my knees, uncaring that I'd landed in the slushy remains of the small snowfall we'd had earlier today. The action was automatic; familiar, yet different. Because this time I really, really wanted this. And I wanted him to look back on this and remember how a bartender with no prospects sucked him off in a dirty alley and gave him the best blowjob of his life.

My hands slid up his hard, muscular thighs, all the way up until I had them splayed out on either side of the huge tent in his trousers. Then I leaned in, running my nose up the outline of his erection, my mouth closing over the tip for a brief moment before I moved back.

"Little cocktease." His fingers slid into my hair, and he tugged, that pleasure-pain combination spiking my arousal again. My underwear was damp with precum and my dick was aching for relief.

I trailed my fingers over his length, drawing a rumbling growl from his throat. He removed one of his hands from my hair and tapped on his watch. I took the hint, unzipping him and easing his cock free. Fuck, it was beautiful—long and thick and flushed, the head glistening enticingly in the moonlight.

"Mmm," I breathed, gripping his thighs for balance as I lowered my head, beginning with mouthing at his balls, fucking high off the scent of his arousal. Sliding my tongue all the way up the underside of his shaft, I licked around his cockhead, savouring the almost sweet taste of his precum as his dick pulsed under my tongue. I dug my fingers into his tense thighs for a better grip, closing my mouth around him and taking him down my throat. He was so fucking big that I had to go slow, but in the end, I was all the way down to the base.

"Fuck," he muttered from above me, both hands back in my hair, his grip tightening. Looking up, I met his dark, hungry gaze. "I'm gonna fuck your mouth now, pretty boy. I want to see those tears."

I was just a hole for him to fuck. The realisation shouldn't have come as a surprise, but it still came with a sting of disappointment.

Maybe something in my expression gave me away because his grip gentled, and he tapped on the side of my head. "Look at me. That's better. You're fucking beautiful on your knees, and you're going to look even better with tears streaming down your gorgeous face. If it gets too much, do this on my thigh—" He tapped the side of my head again. "—and I'll pull back."

That was the only warning he gave me before he snapped his hips forwards, and then I was choking on his cock.

The tears sprang to my eyes almost instantaneously as his cock hit the back of my throat over and over again. I struggled for breath, my tears spilling over and running down my cheeks, my fingers digging into his thighs so hard that I was sure he'd have ten finger-shaped bruises on his skin tomorrow. There was no chance to try any more of my usual tricks to get someone off. All I could do was hang on for the ride and try not to pass out.

By the time he groaned long and low and his dick pulsed, hot ropes of cum shooting down my throat, spots were dancing in front of my eyes and my face was wet with tears. He slid his softening cock out of my mouth, and I slumped forwards, letting his thigh take the weight of my body while I gulped air into my lungs. Chuckling softly, he tucked himself back into his trousers, and then pulled me to my feet. I swayed a little, still lightheaded, so he backed me up against the wall, placing one hand at the small of my back for extra support.

"Mmm. Just as gorgeous as I knew you'd be." His tongue slid out as he angled his head forwards, and then he carefully licked away my tears. No one had ever done anything like that to me before, and it was so fucking hot. When his mouth moved lower, down to my throat, and he sucked a chain of bruises into my skin, I felt like I was going out of my mind. I'd been on the edge for so long, and the drag of my underwear over my oversensitive head was nothing more than a tease as I desperately thrust forward, encountering nothing but air.

"Easy. I've got you." A warm hand slid down between us, over my aching erection, and I moaned. He tugged my underwear down, and then his hand was moving over my cock, hard and fast. I was so on edge that it only took a few strokes before I was spilling into his hand.

"Fuck, that was…" I slumped against the wall, too sated and breathless to bother forming the rest of the sentence. Raising my gaze to his, I watched dazedly as he brought his hand up, smearing my cum across my lips.

"Goodbye, Ollie," he said, and then he was gone.

3

OLLIE

I stopped at the entrance to the fields, taking everything in. Shifting my heavy backpack on my shoulders, I stepped to the left to avoid a group of giggling women. My backpack dug into my skin as I twisted out of their way, and I once again cursed the fact that I always felt the need to carry my worldly goods everywhere I went. I'd learnt from experience that leaving things lying around was practically an invitation for them to be stolen, so I always carried a bag filled with my most important possessions. At work, I stowed it underneath the bar, the one place I was confident it would be safe. The rest of the time, I carried it with me.

Whatever. It was good that I'd brought it with me today. I'd woken up this morning in my tiny, freezing attic "bedroom" to find that my bed was soaked through, from the lumpy duvet to the sagging mattress. All thanks to the third roof leak in less than two weeks. It was something I couldn't complain about, because I wasn't technically a legal tenant, and the attic space I was sharing with three others, our "rooms" split by cheap sheets of plywood, wasn't legally classed as a living space. At least my bag had been protected, away from the area of the leak, shoved under the chair that I propped against the door every night when I went to sleep.

Jai had given me a ticket for this—the Cirque des Masques—as a thanks for covering his shift at work. He was still sick, so couldn't have gone anyway, so here I was, having walked the three miles out of town, trudging through first wet slush, then proper snow as the built-up areas were replaced by fields. Darkness had fallen as I walked, but the entrance to the circus was lit up.

A large painted sign studded with yellow light bulbs and pronouncing the circus name marked the way. Hanging lanterns on stakes were placed at regular intervals on either side of a thick, inky black carpet, a dark slash against the white snow. At the end of the carpet was a large tent striped in red and black—the big top. There was another smaller tent next to it, and off to the side, in the shadows, I caught a glimpse of a cluster of vehicles—lorries, vans, motorhomes.

As I stepped onto the carpet, joining the throngs of people heading for the entrance, I noticed the mist. It was low, curling through the air, licking at the bottom of my calves. For the first time that evening, I shivered, and it wasn't from the cold.

When I reached the entrance, a man was waiting. He was dressed in black from head to toe with a flowing black cape lined in scarlet red, and his entire face was covered by a smooth black mask. I shivered again.

"Welcome to the Cirque des Masques. Ticket, please," he rumbled in a low baritone, and I held out my battered old pay-as-you-go phone, hoping that his scanner could read my ticket through the cracked screen. I crossed my fingers of the hand that was currently shoved into my pocket and held my breath while I waited. After a few seconds, the scanner beeped, and he ushered me into the cavernous interior with a wave of his hand.

The low lighting in the huge tent was enough that those entering could see to find their allocated seats. Tiered seating surrounded a large ring with what looked like a sandy floor lit by spotlights, with a break in the ring where the performers would enter from.

I checked my seat number and found I was about halfway up the tiered seating, almost directly opposite the performers' entrance, and on the end of a row. Grinning to myself, I sat down, carefully wedging my bag half under my seat and half in the aisle, hoping no one would trip over it. This was already shaping up to be a great experience. I'd never had the chance to do anything like this as a child—never had any luxuries to speak of, so this was going to be a first for me.

About five minutes after my arrival, the house lights winked out, and silence filled the big top.

Then the music began, and I was swept away by the show.

It was a blur of colours and sounds, like nothing I'd

ever experienced before. Moments stood out as flashes in my mind.

The crack of a whip as the ringmaster swirled his cape.

The roar of engines as motorbikes criss-crossed each other inside a huge circular cage.

The screams of a woman, pinned to a spinning board, as a man threw knives with deadly precision.

The graceful leap of the trapeze artist, suspended in mid-air for a moment, before being caught by their partner.

The curl of the contortionist's body as they folded themselves into a glass jar.

The realistic-looking blood dripping from the person running haphazardly around the ring with a bag over their head, chased by a sinister-looking clown.

Then...a man who caught my attention from the second he strode into the ring.

He was twirling two batons that were blazing with fire, but that wasn't what caught my eye. It was *him*. Bare-chested, he was wearing leather trousers that showcased his muscular legs and clung to the large bulge between them. Other than the trousers, his feet were clad in chunky shitkicker boots, and his face was obscured by a mask ending just above his mouth, with cut-outs for his eyes and nose. His sculpted torso glistened, and his dark hair was thick and shiny.

A shiver ran down my spine. A shock of déjà vu, almost recognition or familiarity, even though I'd never seen him before in my life.

The fiery batons spun faster than my eyes could follow. Then he launched one of the batons into the centre of the ring where it exploded into a shower of red sparks. He lifted the remaining baton to his lips, and a huge blast of fire shot from his mouth as if he were a dragon.

I couldn't look away.

When the performers took their final bow, I was already on my feet, but not to cheer. I had to find out more about the fire man. Swinging my backpack onto my shoulders, I wobbled on my feet for a second, recalibrating my balance, before quickly making my way down the stairs and out of the exit.

There was something about the smaller tent next to the big top that drew my attention. It advertised a mirror maze and palm reading, among other things. My attention was temporarily diverted, and I ducked inside the tent.

The tent flap closed behind me, and I was suddenly in darkness. Up ahead, a light appeared, and I moved towards it. As I drew closer, it brightened, and I realised that what I was looking at was a mirror. My reflection stared back, eyes wide, hair tousled from the beanie hat I'd been wearing earlier.

A disembodied voice sounded, echoing all around me.

"Mirror, mirror, on the wall...who is the fairest of them all?"

The words faded, replaced with a dark, sinister-sounding laugh. My reflection rippled, distorting, and then reappeared.

I was no longer alone.

Right behind me, looking directly at my reflection, was a clown with a white painted face and completely black eyes with slashes running from above, where the brows would normally be, down to the bottom of the eye socket. Its mouth was red, scarlet and smeared messily around the lips, almost as if it were blood.

It opened its mouth in a rictus grin, and rows of gleaming, sharpened teeth were revealed.

I fucking *ran*.

4

OLLIE

I wasn't scared...or not as scared as I probably should have been. I'd run away from true danger enough times in my life so far that a creepy clown man didn't even rate on the scale. This was all an act, after all. A performance, and as the clown's laughter echoed behind me, I played along.

Okay, okay, I was a bit scared. It was dark, and that clown was creepy as fuck. I kept getting glimpses of its distorted reflection as I tore through the mirror maze, my pace slower than usual, thanks to the heavy bag thumping on my back.

My instincts didn't usually fail me, though, and this time was no exception. Even though I'd never been in this place before, I relied on my instincts, twisting and turning and making split-second decisions, and suddenly I was in a narrow passageway with mirrors on my right and the tent canvas on my left. Despite my heart pounding loudly in my ears, I picked up voices on the other side of the canvas.

"...Dima," someone said, and my already elevated heart rate increased even further.

Dima.

The man from the club.

It couldn't be him, could it? There was no way.

But...I had to check.

The clown chasing me was relegated to the back of my mind as I ducked down, tugging at the bottom flap of the canvas, and then rolling my body outside. My backpack dug into my spine as I rolled, but I ignored the flare of pain. There was only one thing on my mind. I needed to know who this Dima was.

When I stood, I was cloaked in shadows, just the way I wanted to be. No one would see me.

Easing myself closer, I strained to hear the conversation. There was a fire, fairly close to the cluster of motorhomes. Camping chairs were arranged haphazardly around it, and although I didn't recognise any of the figures, I moved closer still.

Someone unfolded themselves from the farthest camping chair, and my breath caught in my throat as he peeled his mask away from his face.

Those beautiful eyes had bored into mine. Had focused so intently on me as I sucked his cock.

"*Dima,*" I whispered shakily.

"Got you," came a low, sinister voice from behind me, and the last thing I saw before I lost consciousness was the fucking creepy clown clamping a thick material over my mouth and nose.

I was gone.

When I woke, my surroundings were pitch black. My heart rate shot up, but I reminded myself that I'd never been in a situation I couldn't get out of.

I tried to move my arms, but I realised they'd been bound behind my back.

Fuck.

"Hello?" I called out tentatively. No one answered, and as I flexed my wrists, only to find that my bonds were securely fastened, I felt a frisson of fear go through me. Shuffling forwards on my knees as far as my bonds would allow, I attempted to map out the space I was trapped in. It seemed like it was a cage of some sort.

A rumble sounded from somewhere to my right, and then a thin strip light flickered on, illuminating part of the space I was in. I was right—I was inside a structure shaped like a birdcage, the framework made from heavy black iron bars. I recognised it as the one that the trapeze artist had performed inside during the show, spinning on a hoop. Now it was my prison.

I turned my head and met black, black eyes.

The clown laughed, exposing those rows of pointy teeth. I shivered despite myself, even as I glared at him.

"Look what we have here," he crowed. "Someone

who's seen Dima's face...and we all know what the rules are."

"Let me out of here now, you asshole," I seethed through clenched teeth, too angry to be scared when faced with his obvious humour at my situation. He bared his own teeth in reply, moving closer to the cage and pressing his face to the bars. I edged away from him, which made him laugh again. Fucking psycho clown.

"You're not going anywhere," he said in a creepy singsong voice. "You've seen behind the mask, and now you can't escape."

What the fuck? Was this guy for real? I opened my mouth to spit an insult at him, but then I realised something. We were moving. I hadn't even been aware at first, still too out of it to focus properly, but we were definitely on the move. Glancing around me, my eyes now more used to the darkness, I realised we were in what looked like a lorry filled with circus equipment. Propped up against the wall closest to the cage was my backpack, and my shoulders slumped a little with relief.

The clown followed my gaze and correctly guessed my thoughts, laughing yet again. "No evidence left behind." His tongue slid along his teeth, and I noticed a red smear follow it. Were his teeth sharp enough to draw blood from his tongue? Stupid question.

"You should ask your dentist for a refund," I muttered, slumping back against the bars but trying not to put too much pressure on my aching arms.

"Don't you like them? I bet you'd like it if I sucked

your cock with this mouth." He grinned widely, and I couldn't suppress my shudder.

"Hard pass. What did you mean about seeing Dima's face? What are the rules?"

"You'll see." Reaching one of his hands into the cage, his fingernails pointed and blood red, he traced a line up the outside of my leg. I stayed very, very still. When he reached the side of my knee, he tapped his fingernail twice.

The light flickered out as he tapped, and I was left in the darkness with a psycho clown scraping his fingernail back down my leg, across the floor of the cage, and up the iron bar on the other side.

"Sweet dreams," came the voice from the darkness, followed by laughter echoing all around me.

5

DIMA

The low rumble of the SUV's wheels on the motorway lulled me into a trance, my mind drifting. Drifting back to that club. My sexual encounters were frequent, and one quick blowjob in a dirty, cold alley shouldn't have stuck in my mind. But I couldn't stop thinking about it...or more accurately, the boy. *Ollie.* He'd been so delicious, so cute and pretty and breakable at a first glance. All pouty lips, big, honey-coloured eyes, and waves of chestnut hair threaded with gold. Not to mention the lithe, toned body that I'd have loved to have taken apart with my hands and mouth if only we'd had the time. But he had a spine of steel, and those honey eyes had a haunted look about them, indicating that he'd had to grow up far too quickly.

I wish I had kissed him.

Fuck. Frowning at the thought, I shook my head. Kisses to me were far more intimate than a meaningless sexual encounter, and I made it a rule to never kiss a one-night stand.

"Dima?"

I turned my head to see Darius eyeing me with apparent concern. In the front, Kristoff's gaze flicked to mine in the rear-view mirror, before his attention was temporarily diverted by Florin, bouncing in the passenger seat as he described to him how he had "cut a pretty heart shape" into the hip of one of our unfortunate victims.

Confiding in Darius about my unwelcome thoughts wasn't on my to-do list anytime soon, so instead, I diverted his attention, lowering my voice as I leaned closer to him, giving a pointed glance towards the back of Florin's seat. "It's nothing. Did you fuck?"

A smirk appeared on his face. "Mmm. Twice, and again tonight before the show. Why, you want in next time?" He raked his gaze up and down me suggestively.

"Been there, done that," I reminded him. Most of us had fucked each other at some point, although I'd stayed away from Teeth, our resident clown. That mouth wasn't getting anywhere near my cock, or my lips for that matter, even with my bloodlust affliction. Now my thoughts were along those lines... "Why don't you invite Teeth?"

"Not my style. I'm not into pain when it comes to my cock. Florin, though...he says Teeth is great at sucking cock. Uses those pointy fangs to give your prick a prick." We both laughed, albeit a little pained, but then he sobered up. "Fuck, Dima. Now you've put that thought in my mind..."

Leaning forwards, he interrupted whatever Florin was telling Kristoff, whispering in his ear, and then Florin's mouth descended on his. By the time he sat back in his seat, I was half-hard just from watching their little display, and Darius was adjusting his sizeable erection in his trousers.

"A little bit of blood play might be on the menu when we reach our next stop," he murmured.

"Fuck, yes. And I'm going to go out and find a willing hole to fuck." I couldn't summon up any enthusiasm, but I was certain this was a temporary blip.

"Ten minutes until our next destination, gentlemen," Kristoff announced, indicating left to exit the motorway. We were somewhere in the north of England now, close to the border of Scotland, where we would head after our next stop.

The headlights cut through the darkness as the SUV rumbled along the country lanes on the outskirts of town, and up ahead I saw the wooden arrow on a stake that indicated our next location. Kristoff turned off the road, steering through the open field gates towards the small cluster of vehicles that had arrived already.

We pulled up, and I headed inside my motorhome to freshen up. One of the security team had driven it up for me so that I could discuss some changes to the show that I'd been working on with Florin and Darius without having to concentrate on the road.

As I was tugging off my T-shirt, there was a knock on the door.

"It's unlocked," I called out, and the door opened. Teeth stepped inside, his face now free of his heavy clown make-up, softening his appearance somewhat... until he opened his mouth.

"Guess what I have?"

Folding my arms across my now bare chest, I stared at him impassively. I wasn't in the mood for guessing games. He got the hint, stepping closer, a secretive smile on his face that immediately had me on edge.

"I caught a little spy red-handed. A little spy who saw behind your mask. You know what the rules are."

My whole body flipped to red alert. "What spy? How the fuck did they see behind my mask?"

"Come with me and you'll see." Beckoning me with his finger, he backed towards the doorway and exited my trailer. Cursing under my breath, I followed him, pausing only to throw on a fresh T-shirt and shove my feet into my boots.

A small crowd of people were already clustered around a cage that had been placed on the ground, and a slow smile curved over my lips. Someone had been spying on me, had they? They were about to discover the extremely unpleasant consequences.

As I drew closer to the cage, with Teeth manhandling people aside to clear the way, I heard a voice, and although I didn't usually feel the cold, the blood in my veins turned to ice.

My eyes met a pair of honey ones, wide and

desperate. Lips, now cracked from the cold and lack of hydration, formed my name.

Fuck. Fuck. *Fuck*.

"Explain," the voice of Judge, the ringmaster, commanded, cutting through the hushed murmurs of the gathering crowd. I listened with dawning horror as Teeth disclosed how he'd found Ollie spying on me, and how he'd heard him say my name.

I already knew the consequences. It was too dangerous for us to reveal our true selves. If anyone knew who we were...if anyone came digging...we were all going down. Why had I slipped up and given Ollie my real name, instead of a fake, as usual?

"Ooh. He's almost as pretty as me. Can I make him cry before we kill him?" Florin bounded up to the cage, sticking his hand through the bars and lightly tugging on Ollie's hair. A low growl escaped from my throat, and everyone's gaze was suddenly on me again.

"Kill me? *Kill me*?" Ollie shouted. "Let me out of here, right fucking now!" He threw himself at the barred opening, stumbling a little, slamming his hands against the lock.

Teeth was instantly there, thrusting his arm inside the cage and gripping Ollie's throat. "I thought I tied you up."

Ollie was gasping for breath, but he still managed to be defiant, and somewhere deep inside of me, a spark of pride flared to life. Not just pride. Arousal too.

"Your...knots...were...fucking...shit," he snarled

41

between gasps, and Teeth bared his teeth, tightening his grip on Ollie's throat.

I fucking snapped, launching myself at Teeth and dragging him away from the cage. The second he was out of reach, I turned him around and punched him in the gut. He wasn't expecting it, and he doubled over, spitting and wheezing, cursing at me.

"Don't fucking touch him," I spat through gritted teeth, forcing myself to step back when all I wanted to do was to pound him into the ground for daring to put his hands on my Ollie.

"Dima. Explain yourself." Judge's voice cut through the white noise. Drawing my hand over my face, I counted to five before I replied.

"The blame lies with me. I met the boy outside of the circus and I gave him my real name."

From the gasps around me, anyone would think I'd committed a murder. Well, perhaps not murder. That was so commonplace by now, it rarely invoked that sort of response.

A small tic in Judge's jaw was the only response I got. "I see."

Stepping closer to Judge, I met his hard gaze. "You can't kill him for something that was my error."

"I can't?" His voice was deceptively soft. "You think you can tell me what to do?"

Holding his gaze, I refused to back down. His nickname of Judge had come about not only because he was our leader, but because he was known to be fair, looking at both sides of a case before making a final judgement. "I will take the punishment in his place," I murmured.

"You care for him that much?"

No. Yes. Ollie should have been nothing to me. Another pretty mouth that had sucked my cock. But somehow, in the brief period of time that we'd connected with one another, he had wormed his way under my skin. I couldn't let him die in cold blood, not like this.

Instead of answering, I bowed my head to the ringmaster in a show of deference. "I am prepared to bear the consequences of my actions."

"Very well," he said. "We shall put it to a vote. Either you bear the punishment, or the boy dies tonight."

6

OLLIE

The man with the whip coiled at his waist called for the onlookers to disperse, leaving only a small group behind who moved to gather around a small fire. One of them was Dima, and the other was the creepy clown. Even without the make-up disguising his face, he still gave me the shivers, thinking of those rows of teeth sharpened to points.

My fight-or-flight instinct was blaring at me. Ever since the clown had dragged me out of the lorry, I'd realised I was in deep shit. This wasn't like my brushes with the law or your common, garden-variety criminals. These were people who talked about killing as casually as normal people would discuss the weather. And my only hope of getting out of this alive was Dima. Why he'd stood up for me, I had no clue. From the second I'd laid eyes on him, I already knew he was someone who had countless meaningless encounters and I was just another in a long line.

Despite my predicament, my mind kept replaying the moment he'd shown up, his electric blue eyes darkening with rage, and the way he'd torn the clown from me like it was nothing. He was fucking beautiful, and he drew me in like a moth to a flame.

Taking a deep breath, I focused my mind, pushing thoughts of Dima aside and concentrating on my immediate situation. My hands were now free, but the cage opening was still locked. Carefully working my fingers through the bars, moving slowly so I didn't attract any unwanted attention, I tested the hinges for weaknesses, then the lock.

"You freed yourself from Teeth's bonds, hmm?"

My head shot up to see a beautiful woman standing in front of me. Waves of red hair cascaded down her back, and beneath the long black coat that was draped over her, a scarlet leotard clung to the ample curves of her lithe body.

Her ruby-painted lips curved into a smile when our eyes met, and she extended a hand, lightly running a finger over mine, where I was still gripping the cage lock. "Vivienne, at your service. Ariel artiste and wife of Judge, the ringmaster."

"Why are you telling me this? If—if it was wrong for Dima to give me his real name?"

Her smile widened, showcasing perfect white teeth. "I sense something in you, and my instincts are rarely incorrect. Maybe there will be a happy ending for you." She paused. "And for Dima. He's rather protective of you, isn't he?"

"We don't even know each other," I muttered.

Something fell to the floor of the cage with a metallic clink as she laughed lightly. "Perhaps you can change that." Turning on her heel, she swept away in the direction of the fire.

At my feet, there were now two small, twisted pieces of metal, almost like paper clips that had been partially straightened out, but thicker. My heart rate kicked up, and the beginnings of a smile tugged at my lips.

I could work with this.

———

Using the shadowed sides of the vehicles, I crept closer to the fire. No one had raised the alarm yet, but all it would take would be for one person to glance at the cage and realise I was no longer inside.

It had been child's play to pick the lock using the tools Vivienne had left me. Lock picking was a skill I'd had for as long as I could remember, and I'd used it frequently over the years. Now I was out, my first course of action had been to make a run for it, but I discounted that for several reasons. It was the middle of winter, the temperature was below freezing, I had no idea where I was, and no means of getting home. Stealing a car was out—although I was technically able to drive, I didn't have a licence, and I wasn't about to risk the police picking me up. The other, bigger reason was Vivienne's words. *Maybe there will be a happy ending for you. And for Dima.*

Was it possible? There was only one way to find out.

The figures around the fire were locked in a heated discussion when I stepped close enough to reach out and touch them. Without thinking, purely following my instincts, I leaned forward.

"Boo," I whispered in the creepy clown's ear as I tapped him on the shoulder, and then darted around to the other side of the fire, crouching down, concealed by the huge wheels of a lorry carrying circus equipment.

The clown—Teeth—let out a roar of outrage, visibly flinching as he spun around, and I grinned to myself. It wasn't quite payback, but he deserved it. I waited for a second, knowing they'd discover that my cage was empty, and in the ensuing commotion I darted forwards, ending up behind the short, cute guy who'd asked to make me cry before he killed me. Fucking psycho.

It was easy work to relieve him of the knives he had strapped to himself. Pickpocketing was a skill that had kept me alive at times when I was out on the streets with no idea where my next meal was coming from.

Back in the shadows of the lorry, I watched, waiting. Teeth was raging, his teeth bared as he slammed his hands against the bars of the cage. A couple of the other guys were running around, hunting in the shadows.

Now only Dima and the ringmaster remained at the fire. I heard the whine of a dog, followed by barking, and one of the men reappeared with two Doberman dogs snapping and snarling, lunging forwards, only to be held back by the heavy chain leashes that the man was holding. The thick muscles in his arms bulged and strained as he fought to keep them under control.

"Ollie. Come here." The command was spoken softly, and my gaze snapped to Dima, who glanced at the dogs, and then right at my hiding place, holding out his hand. How could he see me?

My heart racing, I unfolded myself from my hiding place, and went to him, my bravado fading away with every step I took, until my legs were as shaky as a newborn lamb's. When I was close enough to touch, he gripped my arms, twisting my body so that I faced away from him, and then tugged me into his arms with my back to his chest.

"Good boy," he murmured low in my ear, before raising his head again, meeting the gaze of the ringmaster across the flickering flames of the fire. I was still shaking, and he tightened his hold on me. "I won't let them hurt you."

The steel in his voice and his strong arms banded around my body allowed some of my tension to fade away. Whatever his reason was, this man had designated himself as my protector, and I knew he meant every word he was saying.

The ringmaster watched us both for a long, long moment. Then he unfurled the whip at his side, flicking his wrist. It cracked, the sound bouncing off the vehicles and echoing around us, and a moment later, the group was assembled again. Teeth saw me and snarled, much like the Dobermans were doing, but he didn't make a move towards me this time.

Judge cracked his whip again, and this time it made a different sound. "Heel."

Both dogs whined, settling down at the feet of the man holding their leashes, temporarily docile.

"Florin." He turned to the cute little psycho. "What say you? Punish Dima, or kill the boy?"

Florin tapped his lips, pouting them. "He's too pretty to stay alive. I'm the only cute one allowed here." He widened his eyes, fluttering his lashes. "Can I slice him up a bit first? Pleeease?"

Before I knew what I was doing, I was speaking up. "Oh yeah? What are you gonna slice me up with?"

7

DIMA

Deathly silence followed Ollie's question. Encircled in my arms, Ollie was holding himself tense, waiting for...something.

Caught off guard, Florin's mouth opened and closed a few times before he recovered. "With my lovely shiny knives, of course." He bounded around the circle to us, his hand going to the concealed sheath where I knew one of his knives was kept. I growled in warning, but he wasn't even paying attention to me, his eyes widening as he patted himself. "My knives! Where are my knives?"

"Looking for these?" Deceptively casual, Ollie lifted his hand, splaying four knives out like a hand of cards. My cock was suddenly so fucking hard.

"My knives!" Florin exclaimed with a gasp, his hand flying to his mouth. He met Ollie's gaze, and something passed between them. Ollie's free hand came to mine, curling his fingers around the side of my palm and gently pushing down. I got the hint and released my grip on him, reluctantly, because he was here in the lion's den and Florin was volatile at times.

Ollie took a single step forward and reached out for Florin's hand. He placed the knives in them one by one, while Florin watched him carefully.

"Stop." Florin's hand closed when there was still one knife remaining. "Can you throw a knife?"

"Maybe." Ollie shrugged casually, but as he stepped back into the safety of my arms, I felt a slight tremble in his body. Sliding my hands up his arms, I pressed a kiss to the side of his head, immediately asking myself what the fuck I was doing.

Noticing the gesture, Florin's eyes widened even further. He stared between the two of us for a moment, then snapped his fingers. "I'll make my decision after the boy's test."

"His name is Ollie," I ground out before I could stop myself.

"Ollie. Oliver. Oliver Twist, the little pickpocket." Flipping one of the knives into his free hand, he darted forwards, grabbing Ollie's hand and pressing the tip of the knife to his index finger. A small bead of blood appeared, and my cock hardened even further at the sight, especially because Ollie didn't even flinch. He muttered something about the pickpocket being the Artful Dodger, not Oliver Twist, but when I slid my fingers around his, lifting his hand to my lips and sucking his finger into my mouth, he fell silent. The rich, metallic taste of his blood burst on my tongue, making me groan around his digit. Fuck, now was not the time for this. I needed to get my cock under control until the situation was resolved.

"That was a little taste of what's to come," Florin said, his pupils dilating at the sight of the blood. "Time for your test." He skipped away, returning a minute later, followed by two of the tentmen who assembled our equipment. When I saw what they were dragging with them, I groaned under my breath.

Lowering my head to Ollie's ear, I spoke, too quietly for anyone else to overhear. "If this is going the way I think it's going, I'll need you to stay very still."

"Okay," he whispered just as quietly. There was a pause, during which I heard him inhale a shaky breath. "D-Dima. Which part of this...this whole situation is making you hard?"

So he *had* noticed the way I'd been subtly grinding my cock against his delicious ass. Taking the tip of his ear between my teeth, I bit down, enjoying his sudden gasp. "Mmm...mostly you. Your defiance. Your courage. Your unexpected gestures. Your beautiful face and sexy body. What can I say, sweetheart? You turn me on."

He shuddered. "What about the other thing? You said mostly me. What else?"

"That..." I angled my head, dragging my teeth down the side of his throat. Biting down on his soft flesh, I savoured the feeling of his pulse beating wildly against me. "Would be...the blood."

There was no time for him to reply because Florin was dragging him away, positioning him against the spinning wheel and strapping him down.

His face shuttered, becoming a blank mask, and it made me want to unpick him, to find out everything that made him tick. Who had put that haunted look in his eyes? How could he shut down so perfectly, become so unreadable, like he was right now? How had he learned to pick a lock? How had he gained the courage to stand his ground here when he was vastly outnumbered?

Florin clapped, bouncing on his toes, as one of the tentmen sent the wheel spinning. "Hold still, Oliver Twist," he called. Taking a few steps back, his humour faded away, a look of concentration appearing on his face. He stood, perfectly poised, and then threw the three knives in quick succession. My jaw tightened as I watched the sharp blades embed themselves into the spinning wheel, one by one. Even though I'd seen him perform this act hundreds of times before, it was completely different when it was Ollie up there.

The tentmen brought the wheel to a stop, and after a quick glance, Florin turned to face us with a sweeping bow. "Part one of the test is complete." He then unstrapped an unscathed and flushed Ollie, pulling him close and speaking into his ear.

To my left, Darius flexed his hands, working out the kinks where he'd been gripping tightly to the dog leashes. "They look so fucking hot together. So angelic."

"Yeah, but Florin's the furthest from angelic you can

get," I pointed out. He was right, though. They looked hot as fuck.

Darius gave me a sly glance. "Maybe your Ollie will be the same."

"Fuck, I hope not," I said fervently. One psycho was enough. Darius chuckled softly, but fell silent as Florin switched places with Ollie, allowing the tentmen to strap him down while Ollie stumbled a little, regaining his balance after being spun around. Florin said something to the tentmen, and they moved to either side of the wheel, holding it in place. When he raised his gaze to Ollie, Ollie nodded, taking several steps backwards, shifting the knife he was holding from hand to hand.

"Is Florin fucking crazy? He's letting an unknown throw—" Before Darius could even finish spitting out the words, the silvery knife was flying through the air, embedding itself in the wheel, right between Florin's legs.

Florin laughed delightedly as he was released from the restraints, and as soon as his hands were free, he lifted the knife, bringing it to his lips and pressing a kiss to the flat of the blade. "I vote for Oliver Twist to stay."

"I vote we kill the boy," a voice growled from the far side of the fire. *Teeth*. Of course. Ollie had managed to get the better of him, and he wouldn't be forgetting it anytime soon.

The vote went around the circle of seven, Judge abstaining, as usual; he had the final say when the vote was tied or people abstained, but he preferred that we came to our own decisions. When it had gone all the way around, the votes were four in favour of letting Ollie die, and three against—myself, Florin, and Darius.

My heart fucking shattered as I thought of this beautiful boy's life being snuffed out, and it came as a shock to me, because I hadn't even known I'd had a heart until that moment in time.

Then Vivienne strutted over, all scarlet-clad curves, her long black coat billowing behind her like a cape. "I vote to keep Ollie here."

Everyone around the circle gasped because Vivienne *never* involved herself with the votes. She was always a neutral party—had been for as long as I could remember.

Judge leaned into her, and they conferred quietly while the rest of us shifted restlessly, waiting for the outcome. The dogs were stirring again, back on their feet, their heads cocked, and over by the wheel, Ollie was a lone statue, frozen in place.

The loud crack of the ringmaster's whip broke the tension. "It has been decided. The boy will live, if Dima agrees to the terms."

I bowed my head in acknowledgement, already in agreement before having heard the terms.

Judge was still speaking. "Dima will take personal responsibility for the boy. If the boy steps out of line, Dima's life will be forfeit. We will sign the agreement with a blood pact."

"So it will be done," came the echoes from around the circle. I would have agreed to anything if it meant that Ollie got to live.

"As for Dima's punishment...thirty lashes."

My shoulders dropped. It was a softer punishment than I had been expecting, and I would bear it with dignity.

"Thirty lashes?" Ollie was suddenly in front of Judge, snarling like a feral cat. So fucking cute. "With that whip? That's a human rights violation. You can't do that to him."

"Can't I?" Judge spoke quietly again in his "don't you dare cross me" voice, but one corner of his mouth was twitching up.

Standing up to his full height of five-feet-seven or eight inches, with Judge towering over him at six-foot-six, he refused to back down. "I'll share the punishment with Dima."

"No," I growled out. There was no way on earth that I'd let him feel the harsh sting of the whip as it sliced into the delicate flesh of his back.

"I have a suggestion," came a soft purr. Teeth prowled towards Ollie and Judge, his eyes glittering in the fire. "The boy can work with me. In return, Dima can receive a reduced number of twenty lashes."

No.

"Ten," Ollie countered immediately, glaring at Teeth, and I was so fucking proud of him in that moment, even though I wished he'd never spoken up.

Turning their backs to us, Judge and Vivienne conferred for a while. Eventually, Vivienne stepped forwards, coming to stand in front of Ollie. She cupped his chin in her hand. "Do you understand what it will mean to take this deal? To be with the Cirque des

Masques is to cut all ties with your former life. To become a ghost, moving from place to place, never forming any outside connections, and never, ever breaking the cirque code."

Ollie met her gaze. "Can I have a moment to think about it?"

Vivienne inclined her head, releasing her hold on Ollie's chin and stepping back. "Of course you may."

Those of us around the fire waited silently, although we all knew there was no true decision to be made. If Ollie refused the terms, his life would end. The Cirque des Masques would never let him escape.

Finally, Ollie took a deep, steadying breath, straightening his shoulders as he stepped up to Vivienne once more. "I'm an orphan. I have nothing to go back for. My...acquaintances...just a text to say I'm moving on will be enough for them to forget I exist. If...if you'll have me, I'll stay."

"Very well." She nodded, and then glanced at Florin. "Florin. The ceremonial knife, if you would?"

When Florin returned with the ornate knife, studded with countless precious gems, and rumoured to have once belonged to a Russian czar, we all gathered closer. I stepped up next to Ollie, sliding my arm around him and dipping my head to his ear. "You need to be absolutely sure about this. Once you're in, the only way out is death."

He looked up at me, and his gaze was steady and true. "I'm sure."

Holding out his hand, palm up, he stood, unflinching, as Florin sliced through his life line.

Blood ran down his hand, dripping into the golden goblet that Vivienne held below. When it was done, Florin gave him a cloth to suppress the bleeding, and then moved around the circle, each of us pricking the tips of our fingers with the knife, sending drops of blood into the chalice.

When it was over, Vivienne handed the chalice to Judge, who held it up above Ollie's head. The gold shone in the firelight, the reflection of the flames dancing across the surface. His voice carried across the windswept fields. "Tonight marks a new member of the Cirque des Masques. A new brother, under our protection. Bound by blood for all eternity, from this day forward."

Then he tipped the chalice, the blood running down over Ollie's curls, rivulets of red streaking over his face.

Fuuuck. My cock was pounding at the sight. Nothing had ever looked so good. I needed to be inside him, now.

"Let me take him back to my home," I rasped, gripping Ollie's arm.

"Wait." Judge raised his hand in the air. "I think it's time we told Ollie the story of what happens to those who see behind the mask, and how we choose them."

"Choose them?" Ollie echoed.

"Yessss," Teeth hissed, suddenly much closer to Ollie than I was comfortable with. His face split with a manic grin, showing all his pointed teeth. "How we choose our victims."

Ollie glanced back up at me, his honey eyes wide. "Victims?"

I fixed my gaze on the flickering flames as I replied, so I didn't have to see the look in his eyes when he found out the kind of monsters we truly were. "Yes. The ones whose lives we end."

8

OLLIE

"Perhaps Dima should share the story in private," Vivienne suggested with a warning glance at Teeth.

"Yes. Private." Dima needed no further persuasion, tugging me away from the fire and away from Teeth's leering gaze. He directed me towards the small cluster of motorhomes, one of them set slightly apart from the others. I pressed the cloth to my bleeding hand, the material now stained red, and concentrated on the burning pain instead of the fact that I'd just signed my life away. There was something strange going on here, and I needed to get to the bottom of it, but for some reason, with Dima, I felt safe. Protected. It was weird. We didn't even know each other, yet there was some kind of tangible connection between us.

"Here." Dima came to a stop in front of a large motorhome, all black with red alloy wheels. Pausing with his fingers gripping the door handle, his gaze flicked to me, and then back to the door. "This will be the first time any outsider has stepped foot inside one of our homes."

Conscious of the blood still dripping down my face, as well as the way my hand was painfully throbbing, my mouth twisted into a wry smile. "I'm not an outsider anymore, am I?"

His nostrils flared, his eyes darkening as his gaze raked over my face. "No," he said hoarsely. "Not looking like that, you're not."

My eyes flicked down to the huge bulge in his trousers, and...*oh*. For the first time, I put two and two together. He'd said earlier that the blood was turning him on, but I hadn't thought anything of it because I was torn between being turned on myself by the way he was sucking my finger into his mouth in the most erotic way and *being scared for my fucking life*.

Ushering me inside the dimly lit interior, without even allowing me a look around, he directed me straight to the sink, where he stuck my hand under the tap, making me hiss as the water hit my open cut. "As much as I don't want to wash this blood away, we need to seal the cut, so it doesn't get infected." He carefully patted my hand dry, and then applied some salve from an unmarked jar that instantly cooled and soothed the sting. Then he wrapped my hand with a fresh bandage.

Once that was taken care of, he led me to the front part of the motorhome, where there was a large seating area made up of plush black leather sofas running along each side and two black bucket seats at the far end.

Sinking onto the nearest sofa, he tugged me down on top of him, so I was straddling his muscular thighs.

"Look at you," he rasped. "So fucking gorgeous." His hand lowered, shifting us both, and it took me a moment to realise he was tugging a phone from his back pocket. When he raised it, he snapped a picture of me before I could even blink.

He murmured something low in his throat that sounded like "perfect" before dipping his head to the corner of my mouth, licking across the droplet of blood there. It shouldn't have been hot, not even a little, but my cock disagreed with my brain, straining against my jeans. *New kink unlocked, I guess.*

"Dima," I gasped as he clamped his teeth down on my throat.

"Yeah, you like that?" His words vibrated across my skin, and my cock jerked, painfully restrained.

"I need...I need..." I couldn't fucking think.

"I've got you." Sucking hard enough into my skin to leave a bruise, his hands went to the button of my jeans. There was instant relief as my erection had more space to breathe, despite the fact that it was still confined by my underwear. He rubbed his thumb over the head of my cock, through the damp patch on my boxer briefs, making me gasp as he trailed his nose up my throat. "Fuck, you're leaking for me."

His arms came to my waist, and he manhandled me onto the floor, so I was on my knees in front of him. Climbing to his feet, he gazed into my eyes through his thick lashes, his pupils dark and wide. Dragging his palm across the hard line of his erection, he groaned low in his throat.

"You look so fucking perfect, covered in blood. Chin up. I'm going to decorate your face with my cum."

Fuck. My hand went to my cock of its own volition, yanking my boxer briefs down under my balls, and as he pulled his thick length free, I had to clamp down hard on my dick to stop myself from coming. This was all so fucking new and different, it was making my head spin, and it was already the best sexual experience I'd ever had in my life.

His gaze went down to where my hand was wrapped around my throbbing cock, and he growled his approval, his hand moving faster over his erection. "That's it. Touch yourself as I come all over your pretty face."

When the first jets of his cum hit my lower lip, I was gone. Done for. My dick pulsed, painting my hand and his leg with my release. My eyes fell closed, and if I hadn't been on my knees already, I would've fallen to the floor, because I was shaking all over.

Fingers threaded through my hair, a soft caressing touch, and I felt him shift in front of me, his other hand coming up to cup my cheek. He slid his thumb over my lips, smearing his cum across my skin. "Good boy, Ollie. You were so fucking good for me."

My tongue darted out to suck his thumb into my mouth, and his grip in my hair tightened. I tasted cum and the metallic tang of his blood, and the saltiness of his skin. It should've been too much, but I couldn't fucking get enough. I sucked harder, swirling my tongue around the digit.

His dark chuckle had my eyes flying open to meet his. He blinked lazily, his lips curving into a slow smile as he took me in. "You like that, don't you?" There was disbelief threaded through the amusement in his tone. "So fucking perfect," he murmured, almost to himself.

My eyes fell closed again and I slumped forwards as sudden exhaustion overtook me. It was all so much—my night caged in the dark with a crazed clown, the escape, the circus people, and now this... My head felt too heavy for my neck to support.

"Shit," a voice muttered from far away, and then I felt myself being lifted. "I've got you."

My head lolled back against the sofa cushions, my eyes still closed as I heard the sounds of someone moving around. Something was pressed to my lips as a hand cupped the back of my head, bringing me a little more upright.

"Drink this," the same voice commanded, and I obediently opened my mouth, letting the cool liquid trickle down my throat. It was easier to do what the voice said.

The glass disappeared and the next minute, a damp cloth began stroking over my face. "We need to shower this blood off you, but you need sleep more," the voice said softly. The cloth disappeared. There was a moment when I felt suspended, hazy, like I was dreaming or floating away, but then I felt the brush of the cloth again, this time over my abdomen and then around my spent cock. I dimly registered my jeans being tugged off and a soft, heavy blanket being placed over me, and through the haze a thought pushed at the back of my mind. No one had ever taken care of me like this before.

The thought had barely taken root in my mind when a hand gently stroked down the side of my face, and I was lost to the darkness.

9

DIMA

"Where's the boy?"

"Sleeping. And stay the fuck away from him," I ground out, pushing past Teeth to throw myself down in one of the folding chairs that had been set up around the fire.

"It's not like you to be so possessive." He raised a brow, handing me the bottle of vodka he'd been swigging from, which I assumed was his version of an apology.

"You come anywhere near him, and I'll rip your throat out with my bare hands and feed you to the dogs." My words were low, the threat in my voice implicit.

He took the hint.

"Fine. I'll agree to stay away from your precious possession. Until you get bored of him, that is. Oh, and don't forget that he agreed to work with me in exchange for your punishment being lessened. I'll have to come near him then."

I bared my teeth at him, and he did the same, his sharp fangs flashing in the firelight.

"Dima. Have you explained our circumstances to the boy?" Judge strode over, a bottle of Kraken Rum dangling from his fingertips. He shot me a warning look, and I made an effort to unclench my jaw. Fucking Teeth.

I exhaled heavily, and then took a swig of the vodka, feeling it burn a fiery path down my throat. "Not yet. He's sleeping. It's been a long day."

"Don't leave it too late," he warned me, crouching down to pet the dogs that were basking in the warmth of the fire. They lay there, sleepy and lazy, their tongues lolling out innocently, as if they weren't trained to rip out a person's throat with a single command.

Clearing my throat, I nodded. "I won't. Where's Darius? Florin?"

Rising to his feet, he smirked. "From what I recall, Darius suggested something about going to find a third. Kristoff drove them somewhere."

I turned to Teeth. "Weren't you supposed to be their third?"

"I'm working," he bit out, clearly displeased. As I handed the vodka bottle back to him, I noticed the tablet in his hands, names and faces appearing on the screen as he scrolled down. So that was what he was doing. Identifying possibilities.

"Any good matches?"

Glancing over at me briefly before returning his attention to the tablet, he gave a short nod. "Rich pickings here. We have four, maybe five already, and I haven't finished yet. All orphans. All...tainted." The word came out on a snarl, and I felt my own lip curl in response. Yes, we were monsters, but the ones we chose... they were worse. Our system was rooted in justice, even if it was our own kind of twisted justice. Our chosen ones...they were warped, disgusting excuses for human beings, and as far as we were concerned, they deserved their fate.

He glanced back up at me. "Tomorrow, we hunt for the Chosen."

Tomorrow. That meant I needed to talk to Ollie tonight, to explain our motives. He hadn't had a chance to get used to our world yet.

"Dima." Judge spoke my name quietly, but it was enough for both Teeth and I to fall silent. I turned to him, steeling myself for whatever he had to say.

He met my gaze. "Your punishment. Ten lashes, in return for the boy working with Teeth. Correct?"

"That's correct," Teeth spoke up before I had a chance to say anything, his voice smug, and I knew right then that I would fucking kill him, and drag it the fuck out, if he dared to do anything to hurt my—to hurt Ollie while they were doing whatever Teeth deemed as work.

"Twenty, and Teeth agrees not to harm him in any way, not to touch a hair on his head," I ground out, knowing that Teeth would understand the threat in my tone. Here at the Cirque des Masques, we were a family, but Ollie was *mine* and Teeth had already disrespected him. It didn't matter that I barely knew the boy. He was mine, and I knew it as surely as I knew the sun would rise in the morning.

"So be it. Would you prefer to serve your punishment now?" Judge's hand went to the whip he always wore, coiled against his thigh. "Or wait until daylight?"

I lowered my head in deference to our ringmaster. "Now."

"Very well."

The firelight danced across my skin as I shed the clothes on the upper part of my body, until my torso was completely bare. A cold shiver went through me—partly from the winter chill, and partly from anticipation.

I bowed my back and braced myself.

"Not here. The ring."

So this was how it would be. The ringmaster would make a spectacle of me, as a warning to the rest of the company.

Judge called the head canvasman over with a flick of his whip, and they conferred quietly for a minute or two before he spoke up again. "The tent is ready. Take your seats in the gallery. Dima, in the ring."

The Cirque des Masques thrived on drama, and it was no surprise that as I knelt in the centre of the ring, a spotlight illuminated the darkness, shining down on me. I could see the outlines of the company in the gallery, shifting in their seats and whispering to one another, waiting for my punishment to begin.

A drum sounded, slow and heavy and resonant, echoing around the interior of the big top.

Then the ringmaster stepped into the spotlight,

masked and cloaked, with his whip in hand. He spoke softly, but his voice filled the space, amplified by hidden microphones.

"You are here tonight to bear witness to Dima's punishment. May it serve as a reminder to you all. Never share your true name with an outsider. Never let yourself become attached to an outsider. Never, ever show your face to an outsider within the Cirque des Masques, other than the Chosen. Your punishment will be swift and severe." He paused, his masked gaze sweeping over the gallery, and then he turned to me. "Dima's punishment has been reduced, as the boy has agreed to join us, and Dima has agreed to take full responsibility for him. Should the boy betray us, both their lives will be forfeit. I ask you all to keep your eyes open and come to myself or Vivienne with any concerns you may have."

The voices of the company sounded all around me.

So be it.

The first lash, when it came, was a fiery sting across my entire back that set all my nerve endings ablaze. I was flayed open, burning alive. The ringmaster showed no sympathy as he struck again and again, and although I tried to bear it with dignity, the pain was like nothing I'd ever imagined. I'd seen the ringmaster pass judgement on others, but I'd never imagined it would happen to me until now.

Yet I'd bear these lashes, no matter how painful.

For Ollie.

Only for him.

The whip cracked yet again. I was bleeding, red welts

criss-crossing my back, and that had only been...I'd lost track of the number. But the pain was worth it. Yes...I'd renegotiated Ollie's agreement with Teeth. I wouldn't let him spend any more time with the clown than he absolutely had to, even if it meant that I bore the additional punishment. After all, I deserved it. Ollie wouldn't have been here had I not revealed my true name.

10

OLLIE

Blinking my eyes open, it took me a few minutes to become aware of my surroundings. I sat up, stretching, the thick blanket I'd been covered in slipping off my shoulders.

Oh, yeah. I was here. In Dima's motorhome. A single light above the stove provided dim lighting, illuminating a large area with seating, a foldable table, and kitchenette. To my left was the front of the motorhome, and to my right, I could just about make out two doors which presumably led to the bathroom and sleeping area.

I became aware of the throbbing in my hand, although the pain had lessened significantly, and when I turned to my right, I noticed the glass of water and packet of painkillers next to it. Climbing to my feet, I took two of the painkillers, and then went on the hunt for the bathroom. I decided to make use of the shower, because I couldn't deal with the dried blood in my hair any longer. It was making my scalp itch, and I just wanted to be clean.

De-blooded and wrapped in a towel, I investigated the door at the back of the motorhome. *Dima's bedroom.* Black, rumpled sheets and soft-looking pillows, inviting me to come and lie down. That was what I wanted to do, but first, I needed to find my bag. Being without it had me on edge.

I didn't want to help myself to Dima's clothes, especially as he wasn't here, but it was that or put my bloodstained clothes back on. So without poking through his shit too much, I found joggers and a long-sleeved T-shirt. They were huge on me because Dima was so fucking big...or bigger than me, at least. Shoving my feet back into my battered trainers, I made my way out into the night.

There was no one around.

Freezing in place in the shadow of the motorhome, I scanned my surroundings. The fire was still blazing, but the chairs around it were empty.

Then my attention was caught by a glow of light coming from the big top. Keeping to the shadows, I stepped closer.

When I reached the open tent flap and stared inside, my jaw fucking dropped. And then I ran.

"Stop!" My shout echoed around the tent. I didn't even care about the eyes on me, all I cared about was the fact that Dima was kneeling in the centre of the ring, his back striped with red welts. Vaulting over the low wall surrounding the ring, I launched my body forwards, in between Dima and the ringmaster.

Shocked gasps sounded from the seating area as the masked ringmaster stared down at me. Unease trickled down my spine, but I stood my ground, holding his gaze.

"I count twelve stripes on his back." My voice came out shaky. "The agreement was ten."

Dima startled at the sound of my voice, his head whipping around. His gaze was glassy, distant, like he'd taken his mind to some other place while he received his punishment. He blinked once, then again, clarity entering his eyes.

"Ollie, no," he rasped. "You don't need to see this."

I stepped closer, placing my hand to his shoulder, warm but slick with sweat. His muscles tensed under my touch, but he made no effort to shrug me off. "The agreement was ten," I repeated, turning back to the ringmaster.

"Dima renegotiated on your behalf." Judge's words were clipped, and I swallowed hard, knowing I was treading on thin ice. But I couldn't allow this to happen.

"We had already agreed on ten. I count twelve."

Judge lowered his voice, leaning down to speak softly, so only Dima and I could hear. "Dima renegotiated for your sake. In return, Teeth has agreed not to harm a hair on your head."

"I can handle that psycho clown. I've survived nineteen years on this earth dealing with all kinds of unsavoury bastards; I know how to handle myself." I turned back to Dima, my voice softening as I took in this wild, powerful, insanely beautiful man who was willing to bear this extra punishment. For *me*. "Give me a chance to prove myself. Please."

Dima's gaze flicked to Judge's, and Judge gave an almost imperceptible nod. Dima's shoulders lowered, and his mouth twisted as he shook his head at me.

"You're full of surprises, aren't you, Ollie?" He spoke through clenched teeth, through what I could tell was the pain of the lashes.

Judge spoke up, addressing the assembled crowd, but I tuned it out, only interested in getting Dima out of the big top and into his motorhome where I could—whoa. I did a double take at the direction of my thoughts. *Where I could take care of him?* I'd only ever taken care of one person in my life, and that was me. And equally, I'd never needed anyone to take care of me. But...Dima had. After everything. So maybe this was me returning the favour. I ignored the small, insistent voice that said it was more than that, and got us both out of there.

"Oliver." A soft voice stopped me in my tracks as Dima ascended the steps into his motorhome. I turned to see Vivienne, wrapped in a thick black cloak, holding a glass jar. "Take this."

"What is it?" I peered at the jar as I took it from her hands. Whatever was inside was a creamy colour, dotted with green flecks.

Her ruby lips curved upwards as she leaned closer to me, her voice dropping to a whisper. "It's my grandmother's recipe. A herbal salve. The ingredients are a closely guarded secret, but it has healing properties, and all you need to know is that it soothes and heals without leaving scars...or if the wounds are particularly deep, it only leaves minimal scarring."

Closing my fingers around the jar, my eyes widened. "Wow. Th...thank you."

"You're welcome. Take care of Dima." With a bright flash of a smile she disappeared, and I followed Dima inside his motorhome, closing and locking the door behind us.

Now we were alone.

I didn't even have time to worry or think about what the fuck I was doing here because Dima slumped against the sofa with a pained groan, and my only thought was that I needed to take his pain away. I worked on autopilot, gently pushing him to face the back of the sofa so I could clean his back with the softest cloth I could find, soaked in warm water, before applying the salve. The second I'd finished applying the salve he groaned again, but this time it was a groan of relief.

"Ollie." He cleared his throat. "Thank you."

I swallowed hard. How had my life changed so quickly? But this felt so right. "Anytime."

There were vague flashes after that. Now that Dima was safe and the salve was doing its work, I finally succumbed to the exhaustion and mental drain that had been threatening to pull me under ever since I'd first come to the Cirque des Masques.

Dima, scooping me into his arms. Laying me on the softest bed. Covering me with a thick, heavy duvet. The lights winking out, until all I saw was darkness.

II

OLLIE

"Come with meeeeee," the sinister voice hissed in my ear. I bolted upright, instantly wide awake. The fucking asshole clown was grinning at me with his rows of pointy teeth, standing right next to my bed like a complete fucking creep.

I glanced over at Dima, fast asleep, sprawled on his stomach, all rippling, chiselled lines. My cock jerked at the sight. He was so fucking hot and way out of my league, and I'd spent the whole night with him?

My erection subsided when the unwanted third person in the room pointedly cleared his throat, and at the same time, I remembered what had happened yesterday. My gaze arrowed to Dima's back, and I couldn't stop my mouth from falling open. Vivienne had been right. The marks from the lashes were still obvious, but they looked like they were days old rather than having happened just over twelve hours ago.

"What do you want, creep?" Tearing my gaze away

89

from Dima, I glared at Teeth, making my displeasure clear.

He grinned even wider, his sharp teeth gleaming as he tapped an imaginary watch on his wrist. "Time for you to start your work. Chop-chop."

There was no way I was going to get out of this, and I didn't even want to, because all of this meant that Dima would be punished less. Giving Teeth what I hoped was an uncompromising look, I growled under my breath. "Get the fuck out of here. I'll meet you outside in ten minutes."

One talon extended—his middle finger—as he gave me a mock bow, backing out of the room. I wasted no time in showering and pulling on more of Dima's oversized clothes—I needed to get my bag back today—before exiting the motorhome as quickly and quietly as I could.

"What are we doing?" I tried to keep my tone as bored as possible.

He gripped my arm hard enough for bruises to form, but at my hiss of displeasure, he loosened his grip. Slightly. "Little vagabond. You have so much to learn."

I hadn't even known what to expect, but Teeth dragged me all over the place, throwing out introductions to various circus people as we tore through at lightning speed. When we drew level with the lorry that I'd been held in, I paused, digging in my heels.

"Wait. I need to get my bag."

He gave a piercing whistle, and one of the employees came running over. Jerking his head in the direction of the lorry, he instructed the man to take my bag to Dima's motorhome, before grabbing my arm again and dragging me in the direction of a black truck that had clearly seen better days. Wrenching the door open, he jerked his head again.

"Get in."

We ended up at what appeared to have once been an industrial estate, although it was now abandoned. Teeth parked next to a blacked-out van and climbed out, leaving me alone. I fiddled with his car stereo while I was waiting. It looked like his favourite music was death metal, so I spent a fun few minutes reprogramming his preset radio stations to pop and jazz stations. Hey, maybe it would mellow his mood.

When he returned, he thrust a package at me. "Don't lose or break this. Judge will have your head."

"What is it?" I turned it over in my hands. Whatever it was, it was a box covered in brown paper and tied with string.

"Open it and you'll find out."

"Oh? Is that what you do with wrapped packages? I had no idea."

He gave me the middle finger as I untied the string, but I ignored him. When the paper was finally removed, I stared down at a plain wooden box, painted black. Teeth turned on the engine as I lifted the lid, and my gasp of surprise almost drowned out his angry cursing as Shania

Twain suddenly blared from the car speakers. Nestled in a bed of scarlet fabric was a mask. Smooth, inky black, and perfectly formed, with eye and nose cut-outs, curving at the bottom where it would stop just above the bow of a person's lips.

I carefully took the mask from the box and placed it over my face. It was a perfect fit, like it had been custom-made for me.

"What's this for?"

Teeth ignored me, his pointed talons still stabbing at the stereo as we cycled through snatches of music from the 70s, 80s, 90s and early 2000s.

"Teeth?" I tried again, my amusement fading as his irritation grew. I was pretty sure I could handle him in a battle of wills, but the truth was, I wasn't a match for him physically. Having said that, I'd held my own against bigger opponents in the past, when I was literally fighting for my life. Never underestimate a cornered animal who will do anything to survive. Letting my head fall back against the headrest, I let my fingers stroke across the smooth curves of the mask as I stared out of the window, unseeing.

We pulled into the car park of a huge out-of-town supermarket to the soundtrack of silence after Teeth had given up on retuning his radio. He pulled into a space in the corner, as far from the entrance as it was possible to get.

"This is your first test. Buy everything on the list, and then return to the car. Don't speak to anyone. Pay in cash." Reaching into the backseat, he grabbed something, and then thrust it into my hands. A plain black leather wallet, and...my phone.

"Where did you get this?"

"Vivienne gave it to me. The list is saved in your notes app. Don't even think about trying to run, because I can and will disembowel you if the thought even crosses your mind."

They wanted me to go food shopping as a test? Opening the wallet, I thumbed through the stack of notes. *Wow*. I'd never seen this much cash in one place, not even when I was working at the club. Most people paid by card there. As someone constantly on the move, with very little to my name, the temptation was almost too great. But then I remembered Dima, kneeling on the ground with his back covered in lashes, and my resolve strengthened.

Unclipping my seatbelt, I opened the door. "I'll be back when I'm done. Have fun retuning the radio while I'm gone...if you can manage it." I blew him an exaggerated kiss and left his scowling face behind as I made my way into the supermarket, only stopping to grab a trolley.

Vivienne's list was long...very long. From what I could guess based on the quantity of items, I was purchasing food and various other supplies for the entire company, and that included the dogs. But right at the top of the list, Vivienne had written a little note:

· · ·

Ollie, take some of the money and buy yourself some clothes. ~~Spend however much you need to~~. *Judge says spend up to £150. The clothes will tide you over until we can stop somewhere with a better selection and a lower security risk.*

-Vivienne

I smiled when I saw that she'd purposely left in the sentence about spending however much I needed to, letting me know it hadn't been her decision to give me a budget. But then the rest of her message sunk in. New clothes for *me*? Not clothes from a charity shop? Fucking hell, I was overwhelmed already. I browsed through the shelves in a daze, so unused to having a selection to choose from that I didn't even know where to start. And she wanted to go somewhere with a better selection than this? If that happened, I was probably going to pass out.

Fuck.

I ended up grabbing a pair of jeans, two sets of basic joggers, a pair of serviceable-looking black boots, three plain T-shirts, a hoodie, and a thick, warm-looking jumper. Throwing some underwear and socks into the trolley with my haul, I mentally calculated the total and was relieved to find out that I was well under the total spend limit. Thinking way too hard about it, I added a lounge pants and T-shirt set, which could double up as pyjamas. I wasn't certain what my long-term living arrangements were going to be—I'd crashed with Dima, but he'd most likely want his own space back, and I wasn't about to sleep naked if I ended up sharing a space with anyone else.

That done, I moved on to the rest of the shopping.

An hour later with a wallet that was several hundred pounds lighter and an overflowing trolley, I made my way back to Teeth's truck. He actually climbed out and helped me load the bags into the back—after demanding the receipt and the wallet so that everything could be itemised.

When I was back in the car, I glanced over at him. "Are we going back now?" We'd been out for hours already, and I hadn't even had a chance to say goodbye to Dima before I left.

"Not yet. You're going to order us food, and then we're going to pay a little visit to someone."

"What about the food I just bought?"

"It's minus seven outside. It's already in a freezer, we don't need to get it back to the circus yet."

"Fine." I clipped my seatbelt into place. "What am I ordering?" As much as I disliked Teeth, and he disliked me, I couldn't help feeling that it must be difficult to interact with people outside the circus. What with his teeth and all. He'd make old ladies faint and children cry. Maybe he should look at getting some dentures to fit over his actual teeth.

He pulled out his phone and began scrolling, his mouth twisting in displeasure. "Slim pickings here. We'll have to get burgers."

I'd never been a fussy eater—couldn't afford to be. As long as it was edible, it was going in my mouth. "I'm good with burgers," I said as he backed out of the parking space.

"Lucky. You have no choice."

I rolled my eyes, because this was coming from a person that had clearly never known that gnawing hunger when your belly felt like it was going to cave in on itself, when you had no idea when or where your next meal was coming from.

Not wanting to get into yet another clash of wills with him, I changed the subject. "So, is this my job now? The circus errand boy?"

A sinister laugh fell from his lips just as black clouds rolled across the sky, heavy with a promise of snow. "No. You're going to work in my tent. You're the new fortune teller."

I was *what*? "What the fuck! I can't tell fortunes!" Clearing my throat, because my voice had gone all high-pitched, I stared at his profile. "What happened to the previous fortune teller?"

"It's all smoke and mirrors." He threw his hand in the air before returning it to the wheel as he steered around a sharp bend. "It's fucking child's play. I could do it in my sleep, except for some reason people don't like me telling them their fortunes."

"I can't think why," I muttered, folding my arms across my chest. He laughed again, so I prompted him. "Are you going to tell me what happened to the previous fortune teller?"

"Yesssss." His tone grew low and silky, and I was instantly on high alert. "Let me see...where to begin?

Oooh... Once upon a time there was a pretty little fortune teller. We called her Snow White. Lips as red as blood, skin as white as snow, hair as black as coal. Of course, no one outside the Cirque des Masques ever got to see her beauty. It was reserved just for us. Oh, how pretty she looked bouncing on my cock." He reached down between his legs to adjust himself and I shuddered. That was a mental image I didn't ever want to have again. Did brain bleach exist? If so, I needed it.

Tapping on the dashboard, I pointedly coughed. "Yeah...I really don't want to hear about your sex life. At all. Ever."

"Dima fucked her too, did you know th—"

My arm flew out, my fist connecting with his jaw, and he cursed, swerving across the road before correcting his steering with a shout. "You little fucking shit. Don't you *ever* touch me again," he spat.

"I don't want to hear about Dima fucking anyone else, creep. If you can't tell the story without it, I don't want to know." Why was I so angry? It wasn't like I even knew Dima, and from the first time I'd seen him I knew he was a man that had slept with many, many people.

Teeth's tongue darted out to lick a drop of blood from his lip where one of his incisors had pierced it in the mayhem, his mouth curving into a smug grin. Fucker. He'd meant to get a rise out of me, and he'd managed it. "Very well. Omitting all the juicy details, it turned out that she'd been making a plan to run away. She'd been putting aside small amounts of cash from the money visitors paid her to tell their fortunes, not enough to be noticeable until I stumbled across her little stash after I'd licked her pussy so good, she passed out. It wasn't just money. There were documents. Messages to some fucking woman in Bucharest." He lifted his hand, drawing it across his throat in a swift movement. "So that was that. Snow White ate the poisoned apple, and Florin and I took care of the pieces of her body."

What the actual fuck.

"Pieces?" I echoed, my voice fucking quivering.

"Pieces. Some went to the dogs...mmm...they've developed an unfortunate taste for human flesh. Some, we burnt. Some, we buried. We took care of it."

Fucking hell. I was going to be sick. What had I walked into, coming to the Cirque des Masques?

12

OLLIE

Hours later, we arrived back at the circus site. Darkness had fallen, and with it, another dusting of snow. My mind was still reeling from Teeth's disclosure, and the warnings about me never being able to leave the Cirque des Masques suddenly seemed a whole lot more sinister.

Not only that...we'd spent the rest of the day parked in the freezing cold outside some shitty run-down house, the kind I was all too familiar with, keeping an eye on a shifty-looking man that had gone in and out, and at one point, had grabbed a young teenage girl around the throat so hard, I'd opened my truck door before I even had a chance to process my thoughts. Fucking wanker. All that had been on my mind was for me to tear him away from the girl, but Teeth had other ideas. He'd held me down, stopping me from getting out of the truck, and told me to wait.

My head was still spinning after everything that had

happened. I didn't even know how I was going to face Dima and stay composed, but in a stroke of luck, Teeth put some of the tentmen to work unloading our supplies while he directed me to a shadowed part of the big top, where I could watch tonight's show—wearing my new mask. It appeared that I wasn't expected to begin my role as a fortune teller yet, which I was glad of. There was no way I was in the right frame of mind to attempt something like that.

The way the mask moulded to my face, combined with whatever lightweight but strong material it was made from, meant that I barely noticed I was wearing it. I paid extra attention to the acts this time around—now that I'd met a number of the performers, the show had become even more intriguing to me.

Dima commanded every second of my attention as he controlled the fire like a master. Fiery whips flew through the air, arcing over his head, sending glittering sparks falling all around him. His body moved smoothly and effortlessly, powerful and athletic, avoiding the flames by the narrowest margins as he sent the glowing ropes around himself. His torso glistened, making my mouth fucking water and my dick hard, and his mask only drew attention to the full curves of his lips. He was someone beyond my wildest imagination, and how the fuck had I even ended up on his radar?

When the spotlights abruptly winked out in the two-second pause before the final act, I took a deep, shuddering breath, realising that my heart was pounding out of my chest. It felt like the adrenaline had been building all day, and now I needed to do something to release it.

Fight or fuck. That had worked in the past.

Except I'd never cared for anyone that had fucked me before. Not even a little bit.

Did I care about Dima? I barely knew the man. But I'd already made the choice to do what I'd done with him without any form of monetary compensation. That already put him leagues above 90 percent of my previous sexual experiences.

The final act of the night began, but I barely paid it any attention, lost in my thoughts.

"Come with meeee."

A voice I was getting uncomfortably familiar with hissed in my ear, right before the house lights went up, and I made my way out of the big top before the crowd. There wasn't even a chance for me to take a breath of the freezing night air before I was dragged around the back of the tent, not in the direction of the fire, but to a clearing that had been marked out in the snowy ground, a short distance from the circus site.

"Just a little while, and you can meet the Chosen." Teeth grinned widely, rubbing his hands together. His nails scraped over each other, a harsh sound in the otherwise quiet night.

I didn't even want to ask, but I needed to know. "The Chosen?"

"Yessss. The Chosen. You helped to pick him."

"I what? What are you talking about?"

Before Teeth could reply, Florin bounded over to us,

all bright, excitable energy, and I couldn't help the smile that pulled at my lips, even though I felt like I was balancing on a knife-edge with my sanity. He launched himself up onto his toes, placing a kiss to Teeth's cheek, before coming over to me, running his hands over the mask that covered my face.

"Oooh. Pretty. Maurice is the best, isn't he? You look so lovely."

"Maurice?" I echoed.

"Mmhmm. He makes all our masks. He's so talented." He glanced over at Teeth, whose face was free of clown make-up. "Speaking of masks...you should put yours back on before Judge sees you."

They both pulled masks over their faces and lifted the hoods of their cloaks, leaving their masked faces in shadow. It suddenly felt like some kind of creepy ritual moment, of the sort I'd read about but never imagined existed in reality.

Florin's hand dipped inside his cloak, and then reappeared, the now familiar glint of the metal blade shining in the moonlight. He smiled and mimed kissing the tip of the blade, his mask covering his lips. "Nice and sharp, all ready for him."

"Him?" It felt like I was repeating everything he was saying. Dread was rising up inside me, buoyed by the thoughts of the Snow White woman who, according to Teeth, had been *dismembered*.

"Yes. The Chosen. You saw him earlier, didn't you?" He cocked his head at me.

"Can someone please tell me what the fuck is going on?" I hissed through my teeth.

Neither of them replied, and before I could question them again, we were suddenly joined by an influx of circus people. Darius led the charge, dragging a bound and gagged figure with him. The dogs snapped and snarled at the figure's heels, ensuring they kept moving. When they were dumped in the centre of the clearing, booted feet connecting with their body, bile rose in my throat. What the fuck was happening?

"Chosen. You are here to face the consequences of your transgressions," Darius boomed. Out of the corner of my eye, I noticed Judge standing a little way from the rest of us, his arm wrapped around Vivienne's waist as both of them took in the proceedings with clinical expressions.

"You have lied." At that word, a shout went up from the assembled company.

"Cheated." A louder shout.

"Abused." The shout became a roar.

"*Raped*." The roar became a tidal wave.

And when he added the words "underage" and "children" I was baying for his blood right along with everyone else, finally recognising him as the man I'd seen with Teeth earlier, the man who'd been choking the young girl.

As one, the company removed their masks, letting the man see their faces.

Florin darted forwards, flicking his knife in a perfect

arc. Scarlet sprayed across the snowy ground as the man slumped to the floor, the life draining from his eyes.

Then the dismembering began, and as much as I wished death upon the man after what he'd done, I had to turn away. I was going to throw up.

Fuck.

I had to get out of here.

Turning on my heel, I ran. And ran. And ran.

13

OLLIE

"Ollie!"

The shout from behind me made my legs pump even faster, my heart beating out of my chest as I tore through the pitch-black icy fields. The frozen grass crunched under my feet, my rapid breaths sending fleeting clouds in front of my face.

"Ollie! Stop!"

My foot slipped and skidded on a patch of ice, and then I was falling. Down, down, down.

"I don't want any part of your murder circus," I fucking sobbed, completely broken, curling into a ball on the frozen ground. "I can't do it."

"Ollie." Dima's voice was soft as his hand came to my head, his fingers sliding through my waves. "I'm sorry. I wanted to explain everything before this happened, so you could be prepared. I meant to explain, but Teeth kept you out all day...I know it's no excuse."

My mind couldn't make sense of his words, the shock too great. My ears were ringing, and my body wouldn't stop shaking. I thought I'd been through a lot of shit in my life, but nothing could have ever prepared me for this.

Dima's arms came around me, and he helped me to my feet. "Lean on me," he commanded in that same soft voice, as if he was speaking to a wounded animal, which I guess wasn't too far wrong.

"I can't be here," I whispered. "This is...this is wrong. Don't you see that?"

Coming to a stop, he pulled me into him. "Let's go inside where we can talk, okay?"

I recoiled from him, my eyes flying open in shock as I felt the unmistakeable press of his erection against me. "You're *hard*? *Now*?"

"Fuck," he muttered under his breath, scrubbing his hand over his face. The softness disappeared from his voice. "We need to talk. There are things I need to explain to you. Now."

"I'm not going to fuck you or suck you or do anything with your dick, so fucking forget it." Taking a step back from him, then another, I folded my arms across my chest as a barrier against his body.

"I wasn't expecting you to." A muscle ticked in his jaw. "Now come with me, so I can explain a few things." Gripping my arm, he marched me towards his motorhome. I pushed against him, trying to twist out of his grip, but his hold on me was too tight. When we reached the door, he more or less lifted me inside, slamming the door behind us and pointedly locking it.

Defeated, I sank onto one of the sofas, staring down at my hands, which were still shaking. "Okay. Fine. Talk."

He took a seat across from me, his boots appearing in my line of vision, and I was glad that he'd chosen to give me some space. Silence stretched between us, until he finally cleared his throat. "Ollie. The bloodlust...it's an affliction. A disease. I can't help my cock getting hard at the sight of blood, and it drives me fucking insane until I find something...some*one* to take the edge off. I mentioned a little of this to you before, but I want you to know that it's something I can't control." His voice lowered. "I sometimes think...I don't want to control it."

I remained silent, because what the fuck was I supposed to say to that? Jerking my head in a short nod, to let him know I was ready for him to continue, I clenched my fists on top of my knees, my nails digging into my palms.

"As for what happened tonight...it happens almost every time we stop at a new place. This is something that has been happening ever since the Cirque des Masques was first formed. We...no, the founders...they had a vision."

A faraway expression entered his gaze as he stared, unseeing, remembering.

"A long time ago, back in the 1100s, the cirque came into being. It all began with a boy and a girl. They were in love. Desperately. Powerfully. Their parents refused to let them be together because the boy was poor. He was a farmer's son, far beneath the daughter of a nobleman, or so the story goes. One day, the boy and girl met in secret in a meadow of poppies, half a day's horse ride away from the girl's estate. The sun shone down on them as the scarlet blooms danced in the breeze."

He glanced over at me to find my gaze fixated on him, and the beginnings of a smile pulled at his lips before he continued. "They lay in the sun, talking about their dreams. Both agreed that if they were to do whatever they wanted to do with no repercussions, they would join the circus. A small travelling circus passed through their provincial town every year, and both were enamoured by the sight. There were jugglers, fortune tellers, entertainment unlike anything they'd ever seen before."

"They were allowed to go?" I interrupted him, fully invested in the story.

He shook his head. "No. Not the girl. She proclaimed an interest in the weekly market in the castle courtyard, and that was where she stole moments with the boy. When the circus was in town, they would arrange a clandestine rendezvous and she would sneak out, past the guards, as silent as a shadow. One day, they visited the forbidden circus together and met with a fortune teller. She told them that death was in their future, that their roads would diverge, and fate would balance the scales."

Fuck, I realised I was leaning so far forwards that I was in danger of face-planting the floor. Shifting back in my seat, I unclenched my fists, stretching out my cramped fingers. "So what happened?"

"Time passed, and they grew up."

"That wasn't it, surely?" I stared at him, and his lips curved upwards a little more before his smile fell away.

"No. Going back to the meadow, where our history truly began, the boy made a discovery. Rolling onto his side, he reached for the girl, and the instant he placed his hand over her ribs, she cried out. The boy was instantly concerned, and after coaxing the girl, he discovered bruises and lacerations all over her body. She had never let him so close before, always afraid that he would discover her secret."

"Which was?" I couldn't even fucking breathe, I was so invested.

"Her father had been beating her. Quite badly, or so the story goes. Hidden underneath her noblewoman's garments, her body was covered with a near-constant pattern of welts and marks, proof of her father's violence towards her. It is said that when her body was examined after her eventual death, they found evidence of multiple broken bones, a number of which had never healed properly." His voice hardened. "Her father was a very, very bad man, who deserved to be punished for his wrongdoings."

Fucking hell. I swallowed hard. "What happened then?"

"The boy and the girl made an agreement that day. They would run away and join the circus, staying constantly on the move, so the girl's father could never find them. As legend tells, they made a plan to meet outside the town's boundary at the time the circus was due to leave, so they could make their escape with them. Unfortunately, servants can be bought for a price." His mouth twisted. "A stable hand overheard their plans and told the girl's father. He was livid, as you can imagine. He made a plan of his own, sending another servant to entrap the boy, acting as if he were speaking on behalf of the girl. When the boy arrived at the nobleman's estate, utterly unaware of the danger he was walking into, the nobleman drove a stake through his heart, holding it there until it stopped beating. Then he...the fucking bastard fucking fed the boy's heart to his daughter in a pie."

Fuuuuck.

Dima kept speaking, as if he was aware of both my sudden inability to talk and my need to know the conclusion to this tragic story. "Servants talk. Castle gossip is rife, and the girl discovered what her father had done. She ran from the castle and found the circus fortune teller, asking if the prophecy was indeed true. The fortune teller immediately took her to the circus owner, and together, the three of them hatched a plan. They lured the nobleman out into the woods, far from his home, on the pretence of taking the girl by force. Deep within the woods, the circus owner bound the girl's father while the fortune teller placed a stone inside his mouth before gagging him. Then the girl looked upon her father and tormentor, and drove a sharpened stake through his heart, just as he'd done to the boy she loved."

"And then he was dead?"

Dima nodded. "Yes. They cut his heart from his body as it pulsed with its final beats. After stripping him of his clothes, they left his body to the wolves and returned to the circus with his heart. The circus owner called a meeting with his company, announcing the girl as their newest member. Because the nobleman had been a prominent figure in the region, they agreed to change the circus name and to always cover their faces with masks in order to protect themselves. The heart...that was embalmed and sealed in a ceramic jar, and supposedly it's still the same jar you can see today if you visit Judge and Vivienne's motorhome."

Wow. I didn't even know what to say, except... "So how does this relate to tonight?"

He sighed heavily. "I was getting to that. After the girl joined the circus and it became the Cirque des Masques, they made it their mission to seek out justice, led by the girl. Every town they stopped in, they'd seek out rumours of wrongdoing, of victims who couldn't fight back, and they'd enact their own form of justice. Balancing the scales, as the fortune teller put it."

"So it's a tradition, and you—what? You find people that you think deserve to die, and you just kill them? Without a fair trial?"

His eyes narrowed. "Ollie. Do you think the justice system is fair? Do you honestly believe that the guilty don't walk free, every single day?"

I shook my head violently. "Of course I don't. The system is fucked, I know that better than most people,

115

probably. But who are you to play judge, jury, and executioner?"

He dropped to his knees, moving across the carpet until he was right in front of me. Placing his hands on the leather seat on either side of my thighs, his eyes met mine, his expression full of conviction. "Someone must. If not us, then who? These people have committed horrific atrocities, without consequence. Some of them will never pay."

His voice dropped to a whisper. "Do you know what that man we ended tonight did? He used to visit the room of an eleven-year-old girl, every night—"

"Don't." My voice lashed across the space between us. "I can agree that he deserved everything that came to him." Swallowing hard to stop the bile rising in my throat, I continued. "I'm glad he's dead, okay? Really fucking glad. Is that what you wanted to hear? But dismembering someone in front of me, not to mention your whole fucking murder circus...what if you get it wrong? What if you choose someone who doesn't deserve to die?"

"Sweetheart, no. We never do that." He placed his hand on my knee, and I saw red. How could he touch me like nothing was wrong, like I hadn't had to process an entire fucking murder circus in the space of an evening, let alone everything that had come before it?

"Don't fucking 'sweetheart' me. I'm serious." Fuck. I needed to be alone right now, to process my thoughts. Words came tumbling out of my mouth without censorship, even though I immediately wished I could take them back. "Leave me alone. Go out and fuck someone until your fucking dick is satisfied, okay? Just leave me in peace. I can't even look at you right now."

He stared at me for a long, long moment, and then rose to his feet.

"Fine. If that's how you want it, then so be it."

14
DIMA

Fuck. I folded myself into the backseat of the Range Rover, Darius sliding in beside me while Kristoff eyed us warily in the rear-view mirror.

"You're on the hunt tonight? No Florin?" I dipped my head towards Darius as Kristoff started up the engine.

He nodded. "Florin and I...we're not like that. Not exclusive. We want to bring in other people, or maybe even fuck other people in front of each other when the mood takes us."

"But you're meeting him wherever we're going, aren't you?" I smirked at him, and he chuckled.

"Maybe...alright, yes."

"I knew it." I shook my head with a chuckle. They'd started their "thing" the same night I'd met Ollie, and I didn't know what had happened between them, but this time they'd clicked. Yes, they'd fucked each other before, plenty of times, as most of us in the cirque had, but now they seemed to gravitate towards each other, even when bringing a third or fourth into the bedroom.

"Where's your boy tonight?" Darius raised a brow. "Don't tell me you got bored of him already. Wait...you did, didn't you? You could never be satisfied with just one person."

"There's nothing wrong with Ollie," I bit out, defensive of my boy. Except...he wasn't mine, was he? He'd made it clear that he wanted me to leave him alone, and he'd explicitly given me instructions to go out and fuck someone else. Ignoring the vision of those honey eyes staring into my fucking soul, I rubbed the flat of my palm across my half-hard cock on top of my jeans, groaning at the pressure. It was a fucking tease. It wasn't enough. "It's a new town. I'm looking for someone new tonight."

Darius just nodded while smirking at me, clearly not believing a word I said, but I'd show him. Ollie had told me to fuck someone else, and besides that, we barely even knew each other. We owed each other nothing. I could stick my dick in whatever willing mouth, ass, or pussy I wanted to.

The car rumbled down the silent roads, the headlights cutting a swathe of light through the inky blackness outside. I pinched my brow, my eyes closing. "I explained the history of the cirque to him tonight."

Next to me, Darius blew out a heavy breath, immediately turning serious. "Fuck. How did he take it? That's a lot of shit for him to deal with in one night. We all saw how he ran away from the body."

"What do you fucking expect?" My voice came out low and harsh. "I hadn't explained anything to him, and he had to stand there watching that shit happen. And then—" I cut myself off, not wanting to admit it.

"And then?" my friend prompted.

I groaned. "He noticed how hard my cock was, and he was fucking disgusted that I was turned on."

Darius whistled. "Shit, that could be a problem. Maybe it is for the best that you find another willing person to fuck. If he can't accept that part of you, you're never going to have anything lasting with him, Dima."

"You think I don't know that? Besides, who said anything about wanting anything lasting? That isn't what we do. We fuck, and we move on."

I opened my eyes to see him staring straight ahead, a faraway expression in his eyes. "Not everyone."

"Okay. Not counting you and your sudden attachment to Florin. Or Judge and Vivienne, I guess."

Before I could say anything else, he spoke up. "Dima. Don't downplay what you feel for your boy."

"I don't feel anything other than responsible for the fact that it's indirectly my fault that he's involved in this shit in the first place. If he hadn't seen me without my mask..."

Darius shook his head. "You weren't to know he'd be sneaking around after the show. But that's beside the point. The point is, you do feel something for him. Even if you won't admit it to yourself."

"Even if I did, it's irrelevant. I'll find someone else to

satisfy my needs tonight, and everything will be as it should be."

He shook his head again, disbelief clear in his expression, but he'd soon find out that his assumptions were incorrect.

After Kristoff had dropped us off and we'd entered the club, I headed straight for the VIP section. My gaze swept across the space, and I smiled to myself. Despite the small size of the club, there were a number of potentials. I headed for the bar, debating my options, pushing away the thoughts that were trying to creep into my mind of another bar...another bartender...the beautiful boy who had fallen to his knees for me in the cold and made me see fucking stars.

"A martini," I told the bartender, still scanning the patrons. My cock was ready for action, and I was in the mood for something new. A tall, dark-haired man who looked to be in his mid-to-late twenties caught my eye, standing close to the bar. He was with two other men, one also with dark hair, and the other with sandy waves. The three of them were clad in bespoke suits, standing out amongst the clientele of the club. As I took my time dragging my gaze over his body, his dark eyes flicked to mine, and his lips curved into a knowing smirk.

Perfect. He was interested, and he was nothing like Ollie.

After receiving my drink, I strolled over to the group of three, the man watching me walk towards him with amusement in his eyes.

"Excuse me. I couldn't help noticing that you were watching me."

The man's brows raised, his smirk deepening. "To notice that, you must have been watching me."

"Excuse me. Who are you? We're in the middle of a business meeting." The sandy-haired man interrupted our conversation, and I turned to him.

"My apologies for interrupting. Can I offer you gentlemen a drink?" I flashed him a smile, relaxing my posture to show him I wasn't a threat.

"I think we're finished here, aren't we, Jonathan?" The other dark-haired man spoke up, also smirking.

"If you say so." The sandy-haired man shook his head in defeat, throwing his hands up. "What do I know? I'm just the owner of this establishment."

I cleared my throat, holding out my hand to him. "May I introduce myself? Philip Branson. I stumbled upon your club while I was passing through town on my way up to Glasgow for business. It appears that you run a tight ship—I'm impressed with the service I've received tonight."

The sandy-haired man visibly preened. "Well. Yes. In the trade, are you?" He coughed. "I suppose it's only polite to introduce myself. Jonathan Powell, owner of not only this club, but of the attached gin distillery that produces small batches of exclusive gins. Very exclusive. In fact, the gin in that martini you're drinking comes from our distillery."

"A pleasure." I lifted my glass to him, taking a sip and savouring the smoothness. "Delicious. Unfortunately, my trade is a little less exciting. I'm in sales." The word "sales" was usually enough to make a person's eyes glaze over, and I rarely had to elaborate.

The dark-haired man who had caught my eye discreetly elbowed his colleague, stepping forwards with a smile of gleaming white teeth. He held out his hand to me. "Philip. I'm Rob Long. Jonathan's business partner."

I grasped his hand and shook it, making sure to caress his fingers as he released his grip. It was only polite that I introduce myself to the final member of their trio, although all I wanted was to get the niceties out of the way and move on to the part of the evening I'd been waiting for.

Turning to the final man, I once again held out my hand, my gaze sliding to his to find him studying me with a thoughtful look in his eyes. "Austin De Witt," he said. "Here to procure premium gin for my club in London. I always like to inspect the merchandise in person." He stepped closer, lowering his voice. "I've seen you somewhere before. Does the name Credence Pope ring a bell?"

My body was instantly on high alert. This man knew Credence Pope? If so, he wasn't someone I could easily fool. In fact, he more than likely knew who I was. Credence Pope was a powerful figure, a businessman with his fingers in many pies, with a network of connections across England and beyond. He was one of the scant handful of outsiders who knew some of the faces behind our masks. Judge had a mutually beneficial working relationship with him—on a few occasions, he had disposed of evidence for us, and we had returned the favour by delivering certain items across the country and into Europe when he needed to stay under the radar. While I hadn't had any personal dealings with him— that was down to Judge—I had been party to one or two of their meetings, and I knew first-hand how far Credence's reach stretched.

Austin spoke again, his voice still too low for the others to hear. "Your secret's safe with me, just as mine is with you."

I gave a slight nod to let him know that I was in agreement and then stepped back. Catching Rob's eye, I smiled, slow and seductive. "Ready?"

He nodded, returning my smile with a slow one of his own before glancing at the others with a nod goodbye. Knocking back the rest of my martini, now there were more important things to focus on, I followed him towards the back of the club, dumping my glass on a table on the way.

Beyond a locked door was a corridor that led us to a small office. I slammed the door shut behind me and advanced on Rob, who was leaning back against the edge of the desk, his hard length visibly tenting his trousers. Fucking hot. Reaching him, I grasped his neck, angling his head to the side, and lowered my mouth to his throat.

That was when everything went utterly fucking wrong.

I recoiled, ripping my mouth away and springing backwards as I vigorously rubbed at my lips. The flames of my normally insatiable sex drive were instantly doused. What the fuck was happening to me?

Rob stared at me in shock while I breathed in and out, attempting to regain my composure. When I was sure that I could speak again, I met his gaze head-on. "I must apologise for my actions. I—" I faltered.

Sighing, he gave a small shrug of his shoulders. "I would have preferred it if you hadn't made it so clear that you wanted sex from me and then changed your mind at the last minute in such a dramatic way, but... It is what it is. I'm sure I won't have any shortage of options tonight." He shrugged again.

"It isn't you. You're a very handsome man," I assured him, and I truly meant it. "It...it appears that I may have miscalculated something."

With those words, I stepped back until my hand closed around the door handle. "I apologise," I said again, inclining my head before leaving him as quickly as I could.

Outside, I called Kristoff, and when the Range Rover appeared outside the club, I climbed inside, immediately closing my eyes and leaning my head against the headrest. Fuck. This night hadn't gone to plan. Not in the slightest.

Without opening my eyes, I murmured, "Take me back. Please."

The SUV moved away from the kerb, carrying me back towards the cirque.

Towards my destiny.

15

OLLIE

The motorhome door opened with a bang. I didn't look up, remaining in the same position I'd been in when Dima had walked out on me. When I'd sent him away and told him to go and fuck someone else. He was probably with someone else right now.

"Oliver Twist." Florin's voice held a note of hesitance —uncharacteristic for him, from what I knew of him so far. "What's the matter?"

"Go away," I spat, images flashing through my mind of the last time I'd seen him—earlier tonight, slicing into the man with an expression of pure joy on his angelic face.

"I can't. Judge sent me to you." He sighed. "I'm to lock you in, I'm afraid."

"What?" My gaze flew to his. He immediately peered at me, pursing his lips as his huge eyes scanned my face.

"Oliver. *Ollie*. Have you been crying?"

I grunted a sound he could take however he wanted to. I hadn't been able to stop the tears from escaping, and I didn't even know if it was because of the whole murder circus thing, that it seemed to turn Dima on, or the fact that I'd told him to go and fuck someone else when deep down, it was the last thing I wanted. I *had* needed space, but I'd been cornered and lashed out, saying things I didn't mean.

"What's the matter?" he asked again after the silence had stretched uncomfortably.

"Everything. This whole—" I waved my hand in a jerky movement "—murder circus thing."

"Oooh! Murder circus. I love that." His face brightened, but then fell when he realised what I was saying. "Was it me?"

"Uh. Partly." I stared down at my hands. "How can you enjoy doing that?"

Florin flung himself onto the sofa next to me, shuffling sideways so he was facing me and curling up his legs underneath him. "I just do. Why do you enjoy the things you do?"

Meeting his gaze again, I shook my head. "I don't know. But this isn't some hobby. This is killing people in cold blood."

"Mmm." His lips curved upwards, his cheeks dimpling. "It is, isn't it?"

"But why? Tell me. I really want to understand."

He was silent for a while, deep in thought, and then he flashed me a bright smile. "No one's ever asked me that before. You're the first, Oliver Twist. You know these people are chosen carefully, right?"

When I nodded, he gave me another bright smile, and continued. "Then you know they deserve everything they have coming to them. I don't do all the killing, but I'm pretty and I'm the best with knives, so I usually get my way. It's art. Knowing where to slice, where to carve the prettiest pictures on their bodies. Did you know I cut a heart so perfect into our last Chosen that it brought a tear to Vivienne's eye?" He batted his lashes dramatically.

"Great," I said with zero enthusiasm.

"It was." His gaze turned dreamy. The next second, his expression cleared, and he bolted upright. "Oh! I must tell you about the first time Judge let me plan the whole thing. Our Chosen was a history lecturer at a university. He lured one of the students to his home late at night. We already had him as a potential Chosen on our list because of his history of rape and violence towards female students, which the authorities could never pin on him."

He pulled a face, showing how little he thought of the law, and I could agree with him there. Still, trying to catch all the scum walking around on the streets was like trying to catch rain in a sieve.

"The student in question...she was repeatedly raped, according to the post-mortem thing. Then he put her in the bathtub, where he sawed off her arms and legs—" His voice dropped to a horrified whisper. "—while she was still *alive*."

"What the fuck?" Bile rose in my throat.

"Yes, exactly!" he exclaimed. "She would have passed out from the blood loss before she died, but even so, to sever an innocent woman's parts just like that... This man was as slippery as an eel, and he managed to evade the law until there was a complaint from a neighbour about the smell coming from his flat. He went on the run, but we caught up with him. It turned out that she wasn't even his first victim. And do you know what else we found out?"

"No."

"He had sex with his victims *after they were dead*."

"Fucking hell. That's completely sick and fucked up." A sudden thought struck me. "*You're* not into necrophilia, are you?"

Florin gasped, his hand flying to his mouth and his eyes widening. "Ugh, no! I'm not some kind of sick freak!"

"Okay, okay." Reaching out, I patted his shoulder, just once. "I had to ask. Because of the whole murder thing."

"That's *art*. And it's justice." He was pouting now, his mouth downturned, giving me big, sad eyes so I'd feel bad, the manipulative little psycho.

"Right. Sorry I asked. Carry on."

His fake-sad expression was instantly wiped away, and he bounced a little in his seat. "I begged Judge to let me be in charge, and he said yes. Do you want to know what I did?"

"Not really. But tell me." I was resigned to my fate

now. If I wanted to understand why Florin was the way he was, then I needed to hear all the details, whether I wanted them or not.

"I got Teeth and Darius to tie him to my spinny wheel. We spun him round and round and round—" He made a spinning motion with his hands, almost knocking my chin in the process. "—and then when he was nice and dizzy, I threw my knives. I was just teasing him, letting them nick him here and there. Little places like the inside of his arms, his inner thighs, one of his balls..."

"Ouch."

"That was nothing compared to what he'd done. The saw, remember?"

"I remember."

"Good. Ooh! I forgot. Before he went on the wheel, Dima stripped him naked, and I asked Judge to give him a few lashes, just to make some pretty marks." He beamed at me, and it was an automatic response for me to smile back, even though the last thing I felt like doing was smiling. "After that, I did some art on his body. I carved the names of his victims into his skin so that he'd remember why he was our Chosen. Then I started to slice. A little bit deeper every time. His screams were so beautiful."

There was a long pause, during which the smile fell from his face, and I steeled myself for whatever was about to come out of his mouth next. My mind was already reeling from everything he'd told me so far.

"Um. Dima was involved in the next bit. Him, Teeth,

Darius, and Judge took an arm and a leg each and they all cut at the same time I used my prettiest, shiniest knife to slice his cock off. All that lovely blood—"

"I think I'm gonna be sick," I mumbled, running for the bathroom and making it just in time. I stayed there, hunched over until I was sure I wasn't going to bring up anything else, before thoroughly rinsing out my mouth and cleaning my teeth with the toothbrush Dima had left out for me previously. After splashing water on my flushed face, I made my way back to Florin.

He was sitting very still, his hands folded together on his lap. "Are you okay?"

Giving him a shrug, I said, "As much as I can be, I guess. Can you give me the bullet points of the rest of the story without going into details?"

"But details are fun!" He glanced at me, took in my face, and seemed to think better of it. "Okay. I finished him off, we placed a stone inside his mouth and Vivienne sewed it shut, then we siphoned off some blood for a lovely little cleansing ritual before we let the dogs at the body. I wasn't involved in the disposal of the remains. I don't like to get my hands dirty."

Right.

There was another long silence, which I eventually broke. "Do you ever feel bad about what you do?"

"No," was his immediate reply. "I know there are feelings that I'm...incapable of feeling. I know it's not normal, not as the world sees it. But I don't know any other way to be. I've always been like this. We're all a bit different here in the Cirque des Masques. Maybe that's why we all fit together so well."

"Okay. I...I need some time to think about all of this, and I also need to get out of here, because I can't be here when Dima gets back."

He nodded. "I still have to lock you in, in case you run away again, but I can take you somewhere else. Teeth's place is free; he's at Joelle and Splinter's playing cards with everyone." At my raised brow, he elaborated, "You probably haven't met them yet, but their home is the big one with the blue wheels. Teeth won't be back until tomorrow. Those card games go on forever, and they drink a lot, and then they pass out where they're sitting."

"Oh. Okay, I guess if he's not going to be back." I really didn't fancy being woken up by an irate creepy clown in the early hours of the morning.

"He won't. Anyway, I have the key for the padlock that's going to keep you inside, so he'll have to come and find me. But I'll be far too busy getting fucked by a big fat cock." He beamed again. "I can't wait! Speaking of...I'm already late to meet Darius at the club. So grab what you need, and let's go."

When I'd changed into more comfortable clothes and a hoodie, and picked up my backpack, I followed him out of Dima's motorhome towards Teeth's. Florin stopped me just inside with a hand to my arm. The sad pout was back on his lips again, and his eyes were huge and brimming with tears that had appeared out of nowhere. "Oliver Twist. I understand if you don't want to be friends anymore after what I've told you, but I hope we can still be friends. I like you."

I sighed heavily, resigned to my fate. Making him sad would be like kicking a puppy. A hellhound puppy, at least. "We can still be friends."

"Yay!" He gave a little clap and darted forwards to kiss my cheek, before leaving the trailer.

As the door closed and the lock clicked into place, and I was left alone with my thoughts, I did everything I could to avoid thinking about what and who Dima might be doing now.

16

DIMA

Throwing open the door with a crash, I stalked inside my home. My lust, doused in the interior of the club, had roared back to life as soon as I'd left, flaming higher with every spin of the car wheels that took me closer to Ollie. All I could think about was having him, making him mine, making him fucking submit to me. There were conversations to be had, and I was fully aware that he might not want anything to do with me after tonight, but this connection between us couldn't be ignored. What had happened in the club was unprecedented, and I couldn't ignore the consequences of my actions any longer. It was irrational, it was happening at the speed of light, and I was completely and utterly powerless to stop it.

Oliver was *mine*.

And I was damn well going to make sure that he knew it.

"Ollie," I called, my gaze sweeping across the

interior. There was no sign of him. I checked the remaining rooms—while my motorhome was on the larger side, it wasn't big enough for a person to hide.

Which meant he wasn't here.

I took another look around. Was anything out of place?

That was when I noticed Ollie's backpack was missing.

Fuck.

He'd run again. I should never have left him.

I wasted no time in exiting my home and jogging over to Judge and Vivienne's black-on-black motorhome. My fist connected with the door over and over as I pounded on it, calling out for Judge. From beneath the tented canopy to my left, the dogs began barking.

There was no fucking answer.

Which meant...they were probably at Joelle and Splinter's motorhome. If we weren't leaving here tomorrow and if it hadn't been so fucking cold, most of those who hadn't left the site for the evening would gather either in the big top or around the fire. But on nights like this, the usual way to wind down was drinking and playing cards at Joelle and Splinter's, because they had the biggest—not the most luxurious by any means, but the most spacious—interior.

I yanked the door of Joelle and Splinter's motorhome open, the whole structure shuddering at the force as I stomped inside. At least ten sets of curious eyes swung to mine, but I only focused on Judge.

"He's gone," I rasped.

Judge exchanged glances with Vivienne, and then rose from the table where everyone was congregated, the surface littered with drinks and playing cards. Swiftly making his way towards me, he spoke low and quickly. "How is that possible? I asked Florin to lock him in, in case he was tempted to run again tonight."

"Florin? Where—" My words cut off as I remembered Darius saying he was going to meet Florin at the club. I glanced towards the table, before turning back to Judge. "I apologise for disturbing your night."

Judge lowered his voice. "Is this something you need me to deal with?"

I shook my head. "I need to speak to Florin. I'm sure there must be an explanation for this."

"I hope there is, for yours and the boy's sake. You know what would happen if he were to escape. Both your lives would be forfeit."

Bowing my head, I closed my eyes. "I am prepared to face the consequences."

"Good," he murmured. Clasping me briefly on the shoulder, he returned to the table. I slipped out of the door, closing it softly behind me, and then tugged my phone from my pocket. Time to get in touch with Florin and find out what had happened.

There was no answer when I called Florin's number. Not bothering to leave a voicemail, I called Darius. No answer. *Fuck.* In desperation, I hit Kristoff's number. Thankfully, he answered after a couple of rings.

"Dima."

I didn't bother with niceties. "Kristoff. I need to speak to Florin. It's urgent."

"What's the issue? Do I need to come back?" He was instantly on alert, ready to spring into action like the fucking great security guy he was.

"No. Florin was supposed to be locking Ollie inside tonight, but he's not in my home, and his bag was gone. Before I sound the alarm, I need to find out if and when Florin saw him, and what happened."

"Right." Kristoff's voice was clipped, focused, and I appreciated it more than anything in that moment. "I'm parked down a side street next to the distillery adjacent to the club. He and Darius must still be in the club—Tanner brought Florin here not too long ago, and he's parked right behind me. I will investigate. Sit tight, I'll get back to you as soon as I can." The call ended, and I found myself pacing up and down across the frozen ground, imagining all kinds of worst-case scenarios. The lust I'd had earlier dialled down to the barest simmer, my worries for Ollie overtaking everything else.

Less than seven minutes later, my phone rang in my hand, and I wasted no time in accepting the call.

"I found Florin. He spoke to Ollie before he left, and he locked him in Teeth's trailer." I sank to my knees with relief, barely registering Kristoff's next words. "You owe me for something I can never unsee. The position he was in with Darius—"

"Thanks. I owe you," I cut in, not wanting to waste any more time. Ending the call, I headed straight for

Teeth's trailer, my breath clouding the icy night air as I inhaled and exhaled deeply to calm myself.

There was a fucking padlock on a chain stretching across the exterior of the door, and I didn't have the key. I'd bet anything that Florin had the key on his person. I didn't have Ollie's lock picking skills, so there was only one thing for it. *Brute force.*

I ran for the supply lorry and pulled out the axe. As soon as I was back in front of the padlock and chain, I lined the axe up and swung it as hard as I could.

The metal shattered beneath my swing. I instantly dropped the axe and banged on the door. "Ollie. Let me in."

Footsteps sounded from inside the trailer, and after the longest two minutes of my life, the door cracked open. Then I saw his fucking beautiful face, so apprehensive as his eyes met mine. His body was poised, ready to flee the moment he felt threatened.

"What do you want." His tone was lifeless; he didn't even bother framing his words as a question.

"Sweetheart. Please come with me," I said softly. "Just to talk. Nothing more." I wanted more. I wanted fucking everything, but I had to tread carefully. Needed to get him back into my home where I could be alone with him, to make him understand, and to— No. I couldn't think of anything beyond that. Not yet. For the first time in a long time, my cock would have to wait. It was a struggle that I'd never be able to explain to anyone who didn't suffer from the same affliction I did, but it was comparable to being parched on a hot summer's day and utterly unable to quench one's thirst.

He shook his head stubbornly.

"Just to talk," I repeated. Moving closer, I stretched out my hand. "Nothing happened in that club."

Relief flashed in his gaze before he quickly masked his expression. "Only to talk," he said finally, and I had to turn away so he wouldn't see my own expression of relief.

A moment later he appeared in the now open doorway with his backpack slung over his shoulders. I knew better than to offer to carry it for him—it didn't take a genius to figure out that it was important to him, and he didn't trust anyone else with it.

We walked to my motorhome in silence. When we were inside and the door was bolted behind us, I led him into the bedroom instead of the living area. "This isn't me expecting anything," I reassured him. "I want you to be comfortable and this is the most comfortable place in here. I'll sleep out there; one of the sofas converts into a bed."

It was true, but I was hoping it wouldn't come to that. But Ollie had been through a huge ordeal, and I couldn't and wouldn't expect anything from him.

He gave a small nod, crossing to the far side of the small bedroom that was dominated by my huge bed, and after dropping his backpack, he took a seat on the corner of my bed. Pulling up his knees and folding his arms across the top of them, he dropped his chin to rest on his arms.

He surprised me by being the first to speak. "I had a chat with Florin earlier. He explained a bit more about why you guys do the things you do." There was a long pause before he swallowed hard, exhaling a heavy breath. "I...it's going to take me a while to get my head wrapped around it, but I can kind of see why you do it. I'm not...it's not that I agree with it, but I do agree that those people deserved to be punished. I think...I think I might be able to be okay with it. Not yet. But in the future."

My heart fucking jumped in my chest as I watched the visible struggle on his face, the way he held his body so tense, his eyes brimming with a naked emotion he hadn't even bothered trying to hide from me. What heart? My beautiful boy was surprising me at every turn, making me feel things I'd never imagined were possible. *Real* emotions.

With careful, slow movements, I sank down onto the opposite side of the bed, toeing my loafers off. For now, I kept my suit on, not wanting to make him uncomfortable. "I know it's a lot to take in. But we don't do it for no reason. It's something that has been a part of the lifeblood of the cirque ever since the beginning, and as I've said before, we would never dream of choosing an innocent. We only ever choose those who truly deserve it."

"I know," he whispered, his gaze fixed on the wall. "I—I can understand. But I don't understand why you get...*aroused* by it. I know you said it was an affliction, but I just don't get it."

How could I make him understand?

There was only one way I could think of.

Taking what might turn out to be the biggest gamble of my life, I waited until his eyes met mine again.

"I'll show you."

17

OLLIE

'll show you.

I stared at him, and I couldn't look away. This sexy-as-fuck, powerful man, who could easily force me to do his bidding because there was no way I could escape from him, was watching me warily, keeping his distance. His body was tense, his eyes focused on mine.

Taking a deep breath, I nodded. "Okay."

"You're sure?"

"I'm sure."

As soon as I'd confirmed, he stood and rounded the bed, coming towards me, all lethal, prowling grace. He came to a stop right in front of me.

"Legs down and apart," he instructed, and I obliged, dropping my knees and leaning back a little, my hands pressing into the mattress at my sides. When he moved to stand in between my legs, the hard outline of his cock was in my line of sight, straining against the wool of his suit trousers. My own cock was taking a definite interest, and Dima was going to be aware of that fact any second.

"Now what?" I tore my eyes away from his erection, dragging my gaze up the hard lines of his body to his face. A sexy smirk was curling over his lips, and his eyes were darkening as he stared down at me.

"So beautiful, Ollie." His hand cupped my jaw. "See what you do to me?" He tightened his grip, angling my head forwards until my mouth was poised over the tip of his cock. I opened automatically, and he pushed his hips forwards so that my mouth met his fabric-covered erection. He groaned when I lightly closed my lips around him. "Fuuuck."

I drew back, although he didn't let me go far. "Is this me or the blood?"

"This is all you, sweetheart." His free hand moved to grip my hair, his fingers tangling in my waves as he tugged my head back. "Take my cock out."

I'd been faced with other men before, men who had paid me to be told what to do, to be treated like a doll, like their human fleshlight, but Dima's instructions weren't like that. The low rasp in his voice, the way he was looking at me not just with lust but with something almost like reverence...it was so different. I sat up straighter and dragged my hands up his thighs, massaging as I went, feeling his muscles flexing underneath my touch. He groaned again when I reached the top of his thighs and traced one finger down the solid length of his erection. I teased him for a little longer, rubbing my palm across the head, until he tugged sharply on my hair. Then I let my hands drift to his fastenings, first unbuckling his belt, then undoing his trousers until they were gaping open with his underwear stretched tightly over his cock. There was a damp patch where the head was, and I leaned in, flattening my tongue and running it over the dampness, making it even wetter.

"*Fuck*." His fingers tightened in my hair. "Little tease."

I smiled against him as I lowered his trousers and ran my hands over the muscles of his ass. My dick was so hard by this point, obscenely tenting my joggers, and I shifted on the bed, trying to get some friction on it.

"Not yet," he murmured, his voice so low as he caressed my jaw. "Finish what you started."

Obediently, I curled my fingers around the band of his underwear and carefully lowered it, freeing his deliciously hard cock. The head was glistening with precum, and my mouth watered. But I held myself back, because all he'd asked me to do was to get his cock out. So I lifted my gaze to his to await further instructions.

"Good boy. You're so fucking good for me." He pressed forwards, dragging the head of his cock across my lips. His voice dropped even lower; his pupils so blown that his eyes looked like fathomless black pools. "You make me want so many things I've never wanted before."

Releasing his grip on my hair, he looked down at me for a long, long moment, before drawing back slightly and bending down to press a kiss to my cheek.

"Stay there." Then he toed off his trousers and underwear, before making his way over to a drawer on the far side of the bed. As he walked, he shrugged off his suit jacket, and then began unbuttoning his shirt. When it fell to the floor, I noticed the marks from the lashes had faded even more. The view of him from behind was so mesmerising—all shifting muscles, a broad back, and a tight, gorgeous ass at the top of the sculpted lines of his legs.

And then he turned around, and I moaned out loud. That sexy body, that fucking unbelievably beautiful face, and that delicious, thick, long cock.

"See something you like?" The smirk was back, and all I could manage was a jerk of my head as he came back towards me. When he was back in position again, he lifted his hand, palm flat, letting me see what was balancing on it.

A knife. It was around double the length of my hand, with an ornate, silvery handle and a gleaming blade.

My arousal dimmed a little when I was faced with the reality of what his "I'll show you" really meant, but my curiosity won out. "What's going to happen?" My voice came out hoarse.

"Nothing bad, sweetheart. Would you prefer the cut, or would you like it to be me? It won't hurt, I promise."

For some reason, I trusted his words. Maybe it wasn't that difficult to understand—after all, he'd given me no reason not to trust him, and it was clear we had some kind of connection that went beyond the superficial. I licked my lips. "You can cut me."

His cock jerked, and he fisted it with his free hand, his lips parting as he stared down at me. "Give me your hand."

He encompassed my left palm in his, and then turned it over. Tracing the tip of the blade carefully over my life lines, so lightly that it sent tingles running down my arm, he swallowed hard.

"Hold still."

I stayed as still as I could, my right hand curling into the bed sheets as he sliced into my finger, quickly and cleanly. There was a small sting that barely even registered, and then he twisted my hand again.

It felt like it happened in slow motion. A bright red droplet of blood fell from my finger to his cock, a shocking streak of scarlet against the flush of his skin. He moaned, squeezing my finger, and another droplet fell.

"Look at that," he groaned, his cock fucking leaking precum as he watched the blood smearing over his length.

For the first time, I understood. I made the connection.

This was so. Fucking. Hot.

I'd never done anything like this in my life, had never been able to comprehend the attraction until now. But here...faced with this god of a man with the most delicious cock I'd ever seen in my life, hard and leaking and marked with *my* blood...

I did what my body and my mind were both crying out for. I removed my hand from the bed sheets, curving my fingers around the base of his thick length, and took him down my throat.

He made a choked sound, thrusting forwards and hitting the back of my throat, and then his cock jerked, and I was swallowing hot spurts of cum. It seemed to go on forever, and when he eventually drew back, his legs were shaking, and his breathing was a harsh, unsteady rasp. I blinked away my tears, swallowing down the last of his flavour, and then met his gaze.

"Ollie." He sank to his knees in front of me, placing his hands on either side of my body. His eyes were wide with shock. "I've never come that quickly in my life."

A smile spread across my face, and he returned it with one of his own. "You like that, do you, sweet boy? Knowing your gorgeous mouth gets me going like nothing else?"

"Just my mouth?"

His hands came to my thighs, and he slid them up, his thumbs stroking closer and closer to my balls, and I fucking ached. "Not just your mouth. *You*. Would you like me to do the same to you?"

"Please." I collapsed back on the bed, and he chuckled as he tugged down my joggers and underwear. Sex had almost always been transactional until him, and it had *never* been anything like this before. I hadn't known what it was like to feel this all-consuming need for someone. I'd never even experienced anyone wanting me the way he did.

He freed me of my hoodie and T-shirt, and then shifted me back on the bed so that my head was on the pillows. He crawled over me, and then shifted onto his knees, straddling my body. With a wicked smile, he sliced into his hand, and I noticed his spent cock jerk. When his blood dripped onto my erection, both of us groaned. It was warm and wet, and it was completely insane, but something about the action was so fucking erotic.

"I think...I'm beginning to see why you like this," I whispered. His eyes flashed with fire, and then he lowered his head, encompassing me in the wet heat of his mouth.

My moan cut out when he did something with his tongue that had my balls drawing up, and I knew I wasn't going to last either. This whole evening had made my head spin, and now being here with him, with him trying to show me why he liked the whole blood thing...

A week ago, I was shivering in my attic bedroom, hoping that if I was lucky, I could pick up extra shifts at the bar, and now...now this was happening. With Dima.

His finger slipped down, pressing against my rim, and I gasped. My orgasm shot through me like a rocket, taking us both by surprise as I pulsed inside his mouth, feeling him swallow around me while I came so hard there were spots dancing in front of my eyes.

"Dima," I panted, reaching for him. I needed to feel his weight against me, but my brain wasn't working enough to form sentences. He seemed to understand, though, drawing off my cock after one last lick that made me shudder because I was overly sensitive after coming, and crawled up my body to collapse onto the bed next to me. He drew me into his arms, pressing kisses to my hair.

My eyes fell closed.

"Ollie. My Ollie," he said softly, and then sleep took me under.

18

DIMA

I stared down at Ollie, my fingers stroking through his hair. This was an entirely new experience for me. I'd never held another in my arms like this, never wanted them to stay. What was it about him that made him so different to anyone I'd ever encountered before? What was it that had me so addicted to him? His combination of sweetness and streetwise cunning, yes, that was part of it, but there was something else that spoke to something deep inside of me. Something I hadn't known existed until now.

A thought hit me like a bolt of lightning to the brain. It couldn't be. Could it? That rare, almost unheard of connection Vivienne occasionally spoke of in hushed tones? *Âmes sœurs.*

Soulmates.

No. It couldn't be.

The thought was almost too much to comprehend.

Ollie shifted in my arms, his face relaxed in sleep.

Running my hand down the smooth planes of his back to his delicious ass, I felt my cock stirring again. I hadn't even fucked him yet, and I wanted to, more than anything. I needed to be inside him. But I couldn't be selfish. He needed sleep now. He'd been through so much. It would do him good to have time to rest. With that thought in mind, I carefully shifted him so that he was lying fully on the bed rather than on me, and then drew the covers up over him. Pressing one last kiss to his head, I tugged on my clothes and left the motorhome. I didn't bother locking the door behind me. If he woke, he wouldn't run. I was sure of it.

Judge was passing by when I stepped outside, doing the nightly rounds as he often liked to do, despite the fact that it wasn't his job. The dogs trotted next to him, docile with their master.

I lifted a hand in greeting, and he raised a brow with a tilt of his head, indicating that I should come to him. When I reached him, he blew out a cloud of smoke that curled lazily through the night air, and then flicked the rest of his cigarette away.

"Is everything dealt with?"

I nodded. "Yes. It was a simple misunderstanding."

"Good. Now, while you're here, I'd like to speak with you. Oliver is going to earn his keep as our new fortune teller. I trust that you have no problem with that." He meant: I'd better not have a problem with that.

"No problem."

"It was Teeth's suggestion, and I believe it to be a fair one. The boy will still be working with Teeth, as agreed, but indirectly. They will, however, be equally responsible for the tent. Teeth may ask Oliver for assistance with his clown act, and I have permitted it, as long as it doesn't interfere with his fortune telling duties. He is new here, yes, but I expect him to pull his weight." He paused, scanning my face intently. "I know that he means something to you, Dima. This is why I'm telling you this. If he is to survive here, if he is to earn the respect of the others, then that means no special treatment. Not from me, and especially not from you."

"I understand."

"Good." We came to a stop in front of Joelle and Splinter's motorhome. "Do you wish for the boy to stay with you, or should I make a call? We can have accommodation arranged before our next stop."

"He'll be with me." I wasn't going to let him go.

"So be it." We parted ways, and I made my way back to Ollie.

When I'd divested myself of my clothes and reclaimed my former place in the bed next to him, he stirred, his eyes blinking open slowly.

"Where did you go?" His voice was a soft, sleepy rasp.

"A walk to clear my head. How are you feeling?"

Rolling onto his side, he studied me for a moment, his honey eyes intent on mine. "Better. Can you explain more about the blood?"

I'd do fucking anything if it meant him accepting this part of me. I wasn't prepared to let him go. "Come here." Stretching out on my back, I pulled him into me. He lay his arm across my chest, his head on my shoulder, ready to hear what I had to say. But where should I begin?

"Despite what happened earlier, I don't need blood to be a part of sex. But the sight of fresh, warm blood... it's arousing to me. To most of us, in fact. They say it's a curse, that once you join the cirque, you'll be afflicted. Bloodlust...and an increased sex drive. Combine both afflictions, and after our nights with the Chosen, we're usually all pent-up, on edge, needing to fuck. Needing that release. It's a craving, underneath the skin, a thirst that only sex can satiate."

Ollie was silent for a while, and I let him take in everything I'd shared, willing my cock to behave, because even talking about it was enough to arouse me, and I had a beautiful boy in my bed. But now wasn't the time for sex.

"So the first time we met...you'd just killed someone?"

"Mmm, yes, we had. I needed a release, and you were there, and I knew I had to have you." I slid my hand down his arm. "You stole my attention from the second I saw you."

His fingers trailed lazily over my ribs. "You were hard to miss, too."

"I know. You were eye-fucking me from the first moment you saw me."

He huffed out a laugh. "What would you have done if I'd turned you down?"

"I would have found someone else. Everything happens for a reason, though. Here you are, in my bed."

Tracing my hand back up his arm, I paused, before adding, "Did you enjoy it? Earlier?"

"I...I didn't love the taste of the blood, but yeah...I enjoyed it. A lot."

A smile curved over my lips. "You'd do it again?"

"With you?" Raising his head, he looked into my eyes, his face so close to mine that I felt his breath on my skin. "I would. Will you let me kiss you?"

I drew my hand up, cupping the back of his neck. My gaze dropped to his tempting, plush lips and I knew there was only one answer I could give.

"*Yes*."

19

OLLIE

I melted into his kiss. Dima was skilled, there was no doubt about it, but it wasn't just about skill. It was the way he held me in place, directing every aspect of the kiss, but although he was controlling it, it was so fucking soft and sensual, like nothing I'd ever experienced before. Softness was a rarity in the world I'd grown up in, and kissing for pleasure wasn't exactly something I'd known much of, either. But this man. I could kiss him forever, losing myself in the heat of his mouth, the slide of his lips over mine, his tongue moving against my own.

"Fuck. Ollie," he groaned when we drew apart to catch our breaths. He stared up at me, his eyes glassy and dazed. "Fuck. Need you."

His hands slid down my back, and then he cupped my ass, tugging me on top of him, before pulling my head back down to his. This time when our lips met, it was a clash, tongues and mouths moving against each other's urgently as his erection slid hot and heavy against my own.

He rolled us over, his mouth going to my throat. He bit down, hard, and then sucked at my skin. I growled, digging my fingers into his back, which made him groan against me, so I dug them in harder, wrapping my legs around him as I thrust up, the friction of his cock against mine driving me crazy with need. I needed...I needed him to possess me, to fuck me, to make me his in every way.

"I'm gonna fuck you so good, sweet boy." It was as if he'd read my mind. Lifting off me, he reached for the drawer next to the bed, and when he returned, he was holding a small bottle and a foil packet. "We'll both get tested at the next stop, then we won't need to use this again."

I nodded, staring up at him, my dick jerking as he rolled on the condom and began slowly fisting his cock. He gave me a slow, sexy smile. "Like what you see?"

"You know I do." I bit down on my lip, and I saw heat flare in his gaze as he tracked my movements. "Do you ever do it the other way around?"

His smile became positively sinful as he uncapped the bottle and coated his fingers with the contents. "You want your pretty cock inside me, do you?"

"Maybe." With the fact that I hadn't had much sexual experience that wasn't transactional, and with my size and the way I looked, people normally stereotyped me. Consequently, the small number of times I'd had any kind of penetrative sex I'd usually ended up bottoming. In fact, I'd only tried topping once, and it hadn't gone well. I didn't know enough to know what I'd prefer with Dima. I wanted him to dick me down so hard that I wouldn't be able to walk properly, but the thought of getting my cock inside this powerful man was very fucking tempting.

"Hmm. Well, when you know for sure, we can revisit this conversation again. For now, though..." He lowered his body down onto the bed and closed his mouth over my cock.

My hips jerked up automatically, and he drew off me, gripping the base of my cock and then licking a long line up the underside. I moaned, unable to tear my gaze away from the sight of his tongue sliding up my erection, his eyes dark and heated as he looked up at me.

"Turn over. I'm going to get you ready for me now."

I rolled over, pressing my dick down into the bed, searching for friction. It wasn't enough.

"Hold still." His hand squeezed my thigh when I stilled. "Good boy. Legs apart."

Circling a lubricated finger around my rim, he kissed the top of my thigh, and then slowly pushed inside. I widened my legs, pressing back against him as he carefully worked another finger into me. No one had ever taken this much care before, and it was yet another thing that set him apart from every other experience I'd had.

"The way you open up for me. I can't wait to get inside you." He slowly added a third finger alongside the other two, twisting and scissoring them, and the slight discomfort gave way to waves of pleasure as he stroked over my prostate, kissing and placing soft bites across my skin as he did so. "Fuck. I need to be inside you, now."

"Please." My neglected dick was aching and dripping as I arched back into him, dragging along the bedcovers. I shuddered at the sudden friction.

"Ollie," he ground out, the blunt head of his cock pushing at my entrance, and then he was inside, stretching and filling me, his body encompassing mine until all I knew was him.

I'd never known it could be like this.

He began a slow slide in and out, and I could feel the tension in his body from the effort of holding back. "More," I said, and it seemed to be what he was waiting for because he pulled almost all the way out, and then slammed back in, making my entire body rock forwards and up the bed. I pushed back against him, my hands up against the headboard as he snapped his hips forwards again and again, his cock dragging over my prostate with every movement. Then suddenly he was pulling out of me and spinning me over, his mouth coming down on mine in a hard, biting kiss that I moaned into. He shoved my legs back and thrust into me again, gripping the top of the headboard, his biceps flexing as he held his position. There was a sheen of sweat over his body and mine, and it made his muscles stand out in sharp relief. I just wanted to lick the bumps and grooves of his muscles, to worship him, to make him never want anyone but me. It wasn't a realistic dream, but this was so fucking good, I never wanted it to end.

"You feel so fucking good around my cock," he

ground out, staring down at me with his pupils blown wide. "Hold on to me. I'm going to make you see stars."

I fisted my aching cock as I drank in the sight of him. Precum was dripping onto my stomach, and when I slid my foreskin back to expose the head, I groaned. I wasn't going to be able to hold out for much longer. "Fuck me, Dima. I'm so close."

"No touching," he growled. "You're coming from my cock, and my cock alone."

I shuddered at his command, releasing my erection and locking my hands around the backs of my thighs, my fingers digging into my muscles. His hips snapped forwards again. And again.

And then my whole body jerked and stars burst across my vision, white ropes of cum shooting up my body as he continued to pound me through my orgasm. When he came a moment later with a hoarse cry, I realised that my body was trembling all over, the breath stolen from my lungs at the intensity of it all. My eyes were swimming and when Dima pulled out of me, a noise fell from my mouth that sounded like a whine. I'd never made a noise like that in my life.

Dima chuckled, the sound a little breathless, dealing with the condom and then collapsing on the bed next to me. "Fuck, sweet boy." He brushed the hair away from my eyes and then leaned over to press a soft kiss to my lips. "You're incredible, do you know that?"

I blinked up at him, still trying to catch my breath. His gaze was soft, and there was a smile curving over his lips. Somehow, unbelievably, I'd managed to put that expression on his face. This man, who'd slept with countless people, had been satisfied by me. It was mind-blowing.

"You liked it?" It was a stupid question, but I needed to hear him answer.

In response, he shifted his position and lowered his head to the streaks of cum decorating my torso, and licked up my body in one long, slow movement. "I loved it. You're...the best word I can choose to describe you is *extraordinary*. You're like no one I've ever known before, Ollie. I want to know everything about you. I want you to share all your secrets. To trust me to hold them for you." He lowered his head again, licking and kissing across my skin, before moving back up the bed. He pulled me into his arms, shifting onto his back so I was on top of him. With his arms wrapped around me and his lips on mine, I let myself hope for a moment. Hope that maybe this wouldn't end, even though I knew that with a man like him, there was no way I'd ever be enough. How could I be? What could I offer him? I had nothing.

20

DIMA

"I'm going now." Ollie gave me a smile, which didn't reach his eyes, as he ducked out of the door.

Fuck. Something was wrong, and I couldn't put my finger on it. On the surface, things were going well. Ollie had settled into his new role as the fortune teller, and although he himself rarely spoke of it, Teeth assured me that Ollie was doing well. I trusted Teeth to tell me the truth, because the fact was, he still held a grudge against Ollie for the situation with Ollie getting the better of him when he'd first arrived. So if Ollie hadn't been doing the job to Teeth's standards, the entire cirque would have heard about it. Every night, Ollie would crawl into my bed, curling into me as I fell asleep with him in my arms, and although this was an entirely new experience for the both of us, it felt as natural as breathing. The sex was even better now, if that was possible, because we were learning what each other liked, and there was an intimacy that, again, I knew neither of us had ever experienced before, but now I craved more and more of it.

Ollie had begun to open up, to share details of his previous life with me, and I marvelled at how strong my boy was. He'd lived in squalor, in poverty, had resorted to thievery and sexual acts to feed himself, and he'd never once let it beat him down. He'd never stopped fighting, never given up, had never even turned to a life of crime other than what was necessary to keep him alive. It was almost a miracle considering the lack of role models in his life and the situations he'd been in. When he'd met me, despite his lack of formal qualifications and government ID, he was a reliable employee at the bar, and he'd been studying at the local library with hopes of gaining future qualifications. My boy had wanted to learn skills to get himself a proper job—not just one where they paid in cash, and could be pulled out from under him at any moment. He'd been putting aside everything he could for forged documents in order to be able to sit the tests, a small bundle of cash inside a sock shoved into the depths of his backpack.

I'd told him he was extraordinary, and he was. He fascinated me like no one ever had before, and every day I grew closer to believing those words that had inserted themselves into my brain all those weeks ago. *Âmes sœurs. Soulmates.*

It should have scared me more than it did.

But back to the feeling I had. There was something underneath the surface. Ollie's light, his fire, seemed to be dimming, and I couldn't work out why. I needed to take a closer look.

His fortune telling work generally began around an hour or so before the main show started in the big top, taking advantage of the spectators who would arrive early. We had the maze of mirrors in the same smaller tent to the right of the big top, although the fortune telling area was sectioned off from the mirror maze in its own small, dark corner, surrounded by heavy canvas walls, all in black. The only light came from the flickering candles that were placed near him—two on an upturned box, and another on the table where the crystal ball took pride of place. The ball itself glowed with an eerie reddish-orange light, shimmering and swirling, all made possible by a myriad of hidden LEDs.

When I was clad in my black leather trousers, chunky boots, and heavy black cloak, lined with red silk, I opened the drawer that held my masks. I had two—a smooth, plain black one that fit the contours of my face and a more ornate one that covered my eyes, forehead, and most of my nose. It was also black, with golden stitching in a swirling design around the edges and eyeholes of the mask. It was the more dramatic of the two, but I generally used the plainer mask as, for some reason, it seemed to set the circusgoers on edge. I smiled to myself as I picked up the plain mask, slipping it on. Glancing at the time, I realised that I had around five minutes before Ollie began. Time to go and spy on my boy, to see what was happening in the darkness.

I'd chosen my hooded cloak for this purpose, rather

than my usual one, and I tugged the hood up over my head, my masked face now a shadow within the depths of the fabric. Leaving my motorhome, I ducked into the tent and made for the mirror maze in order to come around the back of Ollie's space. One of the mirrors was in fact a doorway and it led into an area Teeth liked to lie in wait for unsuspecting people.

"Boo," came the soft hiss from behind me as I turned the first corner, and I glanced up to see Teeth grinning at me in the dim light, his rows of sharp teeth exposed.

"Save the drama for the paying customers," I advised him, continuing on through the maze.

He came after me, reaching out for my arm. "What are you doing here? Shouldn't you be getting ready for spec?"

I shook off his grip. "I will be. Leave me in peace."

Another hiss came from his throat, but I ignored it as I reached the mirror with the hidden doorway and pressed down on the top right corner to open it.

"Don't follow me in here," I cautioned, and he laughed, low and derisive.

"You want a piece of your pretty boy before the show, do you? You can't even wait until afterwards? I wonder what Judge would say about this?"

Spinning around, I had my hand around his throat before he even had time to blink. Squeezing, I pulled him closer to me. "You didn't just threaten me, did you?"

With a snarl, he ripped my hand away, his pointed talons scratching across my skin. *Bastard*. "No. I'm not a snitch."

"Good. Now go." Turning away from him, I strode forwards and when I was through the door, I closed it in his face.

Now I was in the darkness, more or less. I could see through the mirror doorway from this side, Teeth's middle finger raised to me and his teeth bared because he knew I could see him, and I found myself smirking at him. My amusement quickly died away when I remembered what I was here for. Feeling my way from memory, I reached the back of the area I was in and closed my fingers around the thick canvas wall at the back of Ollie's space.

Peeling back the canvas enough to afford me an unobstructed view, I peered around the corner. Ollie was there, seated behind the fortune teller's table. I could see his profile, and although his face was mostly covered by his mask, I could see his pretty mouth was downturned and his shoulders were slumped. He idly swirled his hands over the globe in front of him, the swirling light inside reacting to the movement of his fingers, shifting and changing. When I took in more of the space, I realised just how dark and small it was. Had it always been this way? I couldn't recall, but something inside me rebelled at the thought of my boy spending his nights shut away in the darkness, all alone other than the few customers that were looking to have their fortunes told, his light hidden, when he should be out there for the world to see. He'd spent all his life in the shadows, and if anyone deserved to be in the light, it was him.

He should be in the ring. The crowds applauding him

from the gallery, on their feet, showing him how much they appreciated him.

But Judge had decreed that he would be our fortune teller and this was where he'd remain. It wouldn't even do me any good to attempt to reason with Judge, although I would try, for Ollie. If that was something he wanted.

I remained hidden away as a woman entered the room. She looked to be around a similar age to Ollie, maybe nineteen or twenty, wrapped up against the cold in a thick, puffy coat, her blonde curls spilling down her back. When she took a seat, she unzipped her coat, and I stifled a growl. Her breasts were high and round and barely covered by the flimsy excuse for a top she was wearing, and she was leaning forwards, pushing them out and stretching out her hand towards Ollie's...

I was moving forwards before my brain caught up, but Ollie was faster. He withdrew his hand, moving it safely out of her reach, and cleared his throat.

"Good evening. What are you here to seek wisdom for?"

The woman giggled, and I clenched my jaw. "You have a lovely voice. Can I see behind your mask?"

Ollie's foot tapped on a small black lever that I could only just about make out the outline of, my eyes straining in the darkness. A moment later, smoke began to swirl around his and the woman's ankles. His voice lowered. "Mortals are not permitted to see behind the mask. To do so is to invoke the curse."

"O-oh." All thoughts of seduction had clearly flown

from the woman's mind as her eyes widened at the smoke licking at her feet and the deadly seriousness of Ollie's tone.

"What are you here to seek wisdom for?" he repeated. "Perhaps I can ease your mind."

I found myself smiling again. He was good at this. But my smile faded as I remembered how he'd looked before the woman had entered the room.

Lost in my thoughts, I didn't realise the woman had gone until Ollie was climbing to his feet, stretching his arms over his head with a groan. I moved forwards, but before I could get to him, a hand clamped around my arm.

"You're needed for spec," a voice hissed in my ear. "Don't make me be a snitch. You know Judge is going to send someone to find you, and if he catches you in here disrupting the boy's act, then all three of us will be in trouble."

Fuck. Teeth was right. Shrugging him off, I lowered the canvas flap and stalked away, leaving Ollie alone in the dark with only a sadistic clown for company.

Something had to change. I couldn't let the fire inside Ollie die.

I began to plan.

21

OLLIE

We'd reached the north of Scotland. The Highlands had a wild, savage beauty that I'd never experienced before, and I wished we'd had more than a few nights so I could explore them. We were now north of Inverness, which was our next destination, but we were taking an overnight detour even farther north to visit something Dima referred to as "the complex."

He kept glancing over at me as Kristoff drove us to wherever we were going, and I knew that he was worried about me. It was something that I couldn't articulate, but I was simultaneously the happiest and the most anxious and low I'd ever been. It all boiled down to this: Dima made me happy. So happy. And then there were the cirque folk, who, for the most part, tolerated me well enough, or were even outright friendly in the case of Florin and Darius.

Then there were the not-so-happy parts. I knew

about Dima's needs. His bloodlust, and his sexual appetite. He'd told me about them in detail, and combined with things I'd picked up from Florin, Darius, and the psycho clown, it had become clear to me that him sharing his bed with me every night could never be anything more than a temporary situation. I couldn't satisfy him long-term. How could I, when he was used to sex with a different person every night, when he needed to switch things up to satisfy his cravings, when he wanted more than I could give?

That was my first concern, and I knew that if I brought it up he'd do his best to reassure me, but I knew it wouldn't stop my worries. Every single thing in my life had been temporary, so how could I expect this to be any different?

Then there was my cirque act. My fortune telling. I was grateful that I'd been given a chance, and they even paid me a small stipend, not to mention providing me with food, clothes, and accommodation. But being shut in that tiny, shadowy space for hours every day, never getting to see the rest of the cirque, having to trick people into pretending that I could see into the future while avoiding unwanted advances...it was taking a toll on me. I knew I sounded so fucking ungrateful, but it was getting to me, and each day it grew more difficult.

On the occasions I saw Teeth, he liked to needle me, trying to get a reaction, whispering poisonous words in my ears. I could handle him, but it was yet another thing that made the nights feel so long. He still held a grudge, and probably always would. Speaking of Teeth, even he got a reprieve from the darkness—although I knew he loved being alone in the shadows, ready to make unsuspecting customers scream—he got to go in the ring for part of the cirque's second act, while I remained alone in the smaller tent. And I was normally completely alone during that time, because those who wanted their fortunes told were normally here for the Cirque des Masques itself, and the fortune telling was a bonus side attraction.

It was all getting to me, and I didn't know how to make it better. I'd pulled Judge aside after the last show and asked if there was anything different that I could do, even if it was just helping out behind the scenes, but he'd shut me down straight away. It looked like I was stuck here until...until Dima got bored of me, I guessed. And then...I'd be doing the fortune telling without Dima waiting for me at the end of it all. They'd have their Chosen sacrifice after the show, and then he'd be gone, satiating his desire with someone else.

"Ollie?"

I turned my head, almost immediately losing myself in Dima's gorgeous eyes. Every time I looked at him, he stole the fucking breath from my lungs. I wondered when I'd stop reacting to him this way. "Yeah?"

His brows pulled together as he placed his hand on my thigh, squeezing gently. "If something's wrong, you know you can tell me."

"Nothing's wrong," I assured him, holding eye contact. His gaze searched mine for a long moment before he sighed and tipped his head back against the headrest.

"If anything does become an issue, you can tell me anything, okay?"

"Okay." My voice came out as a whisper. I swallowed around the sudden lump in my throat. Why was I being so melodramatic about everything?

The SUV slowed, Kristoff turning the wheel to the left, and we entered a long, rutted driveway, tall pine trees on either side of us throwing shadows across the car. Through the side window, I caught a glimpse of a small meadow with several red deer and an involuntary smile spread across my face. I could make out a mountain in the distance behind the tree line, its peak hidden by low-hanging grey clouds, and to the right, I could see the shimmer of water through the trees. It might've been a loch or even a river.

We drove down the track for what felt like an eternity, travelling in convoy with the other cirque vehicles. Eventually we reached a large open space with a long, low cabin to the right and a two-storey wooden house to the left. As Kristoff came to a stop in front of the cabin, I heard dogs barking, and then the door to the house opened. Three small dogs piled out, followed by a tall, stooped man with a weathered face and a long, snowy white beard and hair, walking with the assistance of a wooden staff. Imagine an old wizard—that was how he looked to me. All that was missing was the hat. And the magic.

When he saw us there, his lined face split into a grin

and he held out his arms. Vivienne got there first, her red hair shining in the weak winter sun as she wrapped her arms around the old man with a wide smile. Judge followed, greeting the man with a bow, before the man laughed and pulled him into a hug, clapping him on the back.

An old woman appeared in the doorway, her long hair pure white, except for a streak of black down the left side of her head, making her stand out instantly. Vivienne immediately moved to hug her.

Everyone began piling out of the cars and motorhomes, greeting the two strangers, while I stared out of the window. "What's going on?"

Dima slid across the backseat and pressed a kiss to the side of my head. "These are our grandparents." At my noise of surprise, he chuckled softly. "Not by blood...for most of us, at least. Judge is their biological son, as is Splinter. The rest of us...some are children of the cirque, but some, they adopted as their own. We were orphans, just children, usually connected to the Chosen in some way, and they took us in and gave us a home. The man there?" He pointed at the old wizard man. "That's Édouard, the previous ringmaster before Judge took over. When we become too old for the travelling lifestyle, or we can no longer participate, or we have children and need to take time out from being on the road while they're young, we come here. This is the complex. Next to Édouard is his wife, Mercy. She was once our greatest contortionist and aerial artiste. She taught Vivienne all she knows."

I blinked, trying to make sense of his words, latching on to the one question that came to mind. "A complex?"

Reaching across me to open the door, he smiled. "Come on. I'll show you."

Everything fell silent as we crossed the space between the car and the two people. As we drew nearer, I could feel my palms becoming clammy, and I made an effort to lock down everything I was feeling because all eyes were on me, and there was a sense of anticipation in the air, like everyone was holding their breath, waiting for something.

The dogs danced around my feet, sending small stones skittering around us, and from somewhere nearby, I heard the sound of chickens clucking, but other than that, the silence was unbroken. Dima had a hand on my lower back, and he didn't move away, even when we reached Édouard and Mercy, although he took the time to bow to each of them in turn.

Édouard stepped forwards with the help of his cane, his piercing gaze on me. "What is your name, boy?"

Moistening my dry lips with my tongue, I cleared my throat. "Ollie. Um. Oliver."

He inclined his head, before stepping back. "Oliver."

I shot a glance at Dima. *That was it?* Dima caught my eye and stroked his thumb in circles over the small of my back, his expression reassuring me.

The reassurance lasted for less than a minute.

Then it was the turn of Mercy. She didn't need to use a cane to walk—if anything, it seemed like she glided towards me. Coming to a stop right in front of me, she reached up and cupped my chin in her hand, turning my head first to one side, then the other. She muttered some words in rapid-fire French that I didn't have a hope of understanding, shaking her head. Beckoning Judge towards her, she whispered into his ear, and his body stiffened as his gaze shot to mine. Fuck. My heart was beating out of my chest. This wasn't good, was it?

Dima must've felt my body tremble, because he straightened up, his voice low and commanding. "I'd like to show Ollie around now."

Mercy inclined her head, and Dima tugged me away from the prying eyes, leading me around the corner of the house until we were away from everyone else.

I didn't have a chance to say anything before he wrapped his arms around me and lowered his mouth to mine. "*Ollie.*"

I lost myself in his kiss. Ever since the first time he'd let himself kiss me, neither of us could get enough. He never kissed me in front of the others, but whenever we were alone, his mouth would be on mine, his tongue sliding against my own, kissing me until both our lips were swollen and red. I was glad for Vivienne's healing salve, otherwise I'd have a serious case of stubble burn going on daily. Dima preferred a shadow across his jaw, and it made him look fucking hot, but it felt like sandpaper against my skin after a long kissing session.

"Ollie," he murmured when we broke apart, placing one hand on the wooden slats next to my head and cupping my jaw with the other. "Don't worry about anything, okay? I'll protect you." Straightening up, he cleared his throat, looking around him. "Come on. I'll show you around."

The house we were currently around the side of was where Édouard and Mercy lived, and the long, low building across from the house was a communal gathering place with a bar, TV screen, and games room. It was also where those onsite would eat the majority of their meals.

Up another path, spread out amongst the trees, were a number of A-frame wooden cabins, and this was where the other ex-cirque members lived, plus several empty cabins for any visitors. The site held a fishing loch, livestock, and poultry, plus an allotment where enough vegetables grew to make the complex mostly self-sufficient, food-wise.

"Is this where you'll end up, eventually?" I glanced up at Dima as we came to a stop next to the small wooden jetty on the loch, where two small rowboats were tied.

"Yes." There was a faraway expression on his face, but he blinked, and it was gone. His eyes met mine, piercing blue and holding me captive. "Are you happy, Ollie?"

"Um." Fuck. I knew he'd noticed that something was wrong, but I was no closer to being able to articulate it than I had been before. "You make me happy," I said eventually. It was the truth, and it was all I could tell him.

His jaw tightened, and he closed his eyes, pulling me into his arms.

We remained next to the loch for a long time, until the sun began to lower in the sky and our surroundings dimmed, and he never let me go. He held on to me tightly, kissing me and running his hands up and down my back, into my hair, down my arms, like he was memorising my body.

My brain was blaring an alarm, my gut instincts telling me to be on high alert. Something about this felt different. *Wrong*. I always trusted my instincts, and the longer we stood there, the more the unease inside me grew.

22

OLLIE

When we returned to the others, they were gathering in a large dirt clearing behind the long building. Wood was piled in the centre, and as we entered the clearing, silence fell. I could feel my body tense, my arm stiff against Dima's, but I kept my expression blank. Hopefully, no one looking at me would know there was anything wrong.

Judge was the first to speak. "Dima. Our hosts have prepared a special treat for us tonight. There will be the usual feast, and after the feast will come the sacrifices."

Sacrifices? Plural? I'd had weeks of being with the cirque now, and I still hadn't managed to bring myself to watch it happen since the first time. I knew it was something that set me apart from the others, kept them from fully embracing me as one of their own, but every time I thought about what I'd witnessed before, my stomach would twist and bile would rise up in my throat. It shouldn't have affected me the way it did, not with the shit I'd experienced growing up.

but it did. And I could guarantee that it would be the same for any person living in the real world who had their life turned upside down and transferred to this murder circus —anyone would have difficulty acclimatising to this new, unique lifestyle. It was something I didn't think any of the others understood. They'd all either been born into the cirque or were orphans who had been with the cirque since they were children. I was the exception, the outsider who'd suddenly found themselves in their inner circle, privy to their darkest secrets.

When I thought about it, it made sense that Judge wanted to keep me tucked away out of sight with Teeth to keep an eye on me. Even when Teeth left me alone to do his creepy clown act in the ring, I knew that one of the guards was always posted outside, and another prowled the grounds with the dogs, always on alert and ready, should I make a run for it. I hadn't yet earned their trust, and the things I knew about them were enough to bring them all down. Not that I would do that. Like I'd said to Dima before, I understood why they did what they did, and I approved of their twisted way of meting out justice, even if it left me sick to my stomach.

"Dima. As our fire performer, would you do the honours?" Judge handed a long whip to Dima, the burnished ebony length glistening in the glow of the spotlights mounted on tall stalks around the edge of the clearing.

Dima inclined his head, accepting the whip. He cracked it experimentally, sending the dogs into a frenzy.

Judge whistled and they instantly fell silent, sinking down to the ground. But I was barely paying attention to them because Dima was taking his fucking top off. I should've been used to seeing him like this by now but every single time, he made my heart race like I'd been running from the law, stealing the breath from my lungs at his sheer beauty. My cock stirred as I remembered kissing down his body the previous night, tracing his hard muscles with my tongue— Fuck. I needed to stop thinking about sex right now.

He glanced over at me, and his brows rose, his lips kicking up at the corners. Amusement glinted in his eyes. I was fairly certain he'd accurately guessed where my thoughts had gone based on his smirk. His gaze dropped to my mouth, then down to the bulge between my legs that was becoming more obvious with every passing second, and then back up to my eyes. Slowly, deliberately, he licked his lips, his hand ghosting over his own sizeable bulge, and my mouth went dry.

Someone cleared their throat, and that was when I remembered that we weren't alone. Tearing my gaze away from Dima, I fixed my attention on the pyramid of wood ready to be set on fire. That was probably the safest place to look.

I couldn't keep my gaze away from him for long, though. Not when he began coating the whip in the oily stuff he used when he set it on fire during his act. There was something so erotic in the way he handled it, his eyes focused and intent, his muscles shifting and rippling as he rolled the handle in his grip, making the length of the whip dance across the clearing.

I wasn't the only one who couldn't keep their gaze away from him, either. Gradually, I became aware of the number of eyes on him, the way people were openly staring, lusting after him.

How long would it be before he got an offer he couldn't refuse? I knew he'd slept with many of the people here. He was fucking gorgeous, talented, powerful, and a good man—he could have his pick of anyone. Even Florin was eyeing him with blatant desire, leaning back against Darius, who was kissing down Florin's neck. It wasn't like I had a thing against sharing, and I knew that most of the cirque members were casual about sex—as I'd been until I met Dima. Sex had never been meaningful to me. But I'd never had anything or anyone that was just mine before, and Dima...he'd somehow become the most important person in my life in an insanely short amount of time. I didn't want to share him with anyone. Ever.

All my worries scattered when Dima cracked the whip again, and flames burst into life, hungrily licking up the length of the whip. He twirled it, fire dancing in front of my eyes as the whip curved into an S shape and then cracked against the ground, sending up a cloud of dust.

He spun around, his body twisting in a sinuous movement, and aimed the whip at the bottom of the pile of logs, where some dry bracken was balled up as kindling. There was an orange glow, and then the bracken was alight, small flames licking at the wood. It soon caught fire, helped by the fuel that had been poured on top, and as Dima spun again, the whip twirling around his body, the bonfire roared to life behind him.

I couldn't look away. He was a shadow, silhouetted against the flames, the whip dancing around him, almost too quickly for my eyes to follow.

It was then that I had my epiphany. My feelings for him went much deeper than the superficial.

How had this happened? I...I *loved* him.

It was crazy, but it was true.

It was going to fucking kill me when he let me go. And I couldn't—wouldn't—ever leave, because it would mean his life was forfeit.

Watching as he gave one final crack of the whip and then doused the flames shimmering along its length, I resigned myself to my fate. What would be, would be. Whatever happened, my life was so much better with him in it, and despite my reservations about the cirque, I knew right then that even if I had the option of returning to my old life, I'd choose the Cirque des Masques with no question.

"Oliver Twist." Florin's whispered words made me jump. I hadn't even heard him coming—I'd been so wrapped up in watching Dima, and my troubled thoughts. This was not good. No one had been able to take me by surprise before I'd come here.

"Yeah?" I turned to face the cute little psycho.

He held up one of his knives, the blade gleaming in the firelight. "Want to play with me later? Rumour has it that there are two Chosen tonight. We could have one each." Batting his lashes, he gave me a sultry smile. "What do you say?"

Before I could reply, he darted forwards and pressed a soft kiss to my cheek. "Don't look so sad. All you have to do is embrace our ways. I promise that you'll love it."

I couldn't deal with this right now. Running my hand down my face, I sighed. "Florin. I...I can't." I didn't even have to look at him to know that his face fell. Guilt twisted my stomach, but I reminded myself that this wasn't my problem. Florin knew how to manipulate people, and I wasn't going to let him manipulate me.

When I moved away from Florin, I noticed something strange.

Dima, now fully clothed again, was standing on the outskirts of the clearing with two bottles of beer in his hands. As I watched, he set them down on the ground and glanced around him. Then he took something from his pocket that I couldn't see, and his hand hovered over one of the bottles. Before I could make sense of what he was doing, Darius moved into my line of sight, blocking my view as he swung Florin up into his arms, Florin's mouth immediately sealing over his.

There was no time to dwell on what I'd seen. Out of the corner of my eye, I noticed Édouard in front of the fire. He brought what looked like a ram's horn to his lips, and a long, low note sounded across the clearing.

Mercy stepped forwards, her arms outstretched. "Let us feast."

23

DIMA

"You look like you could use a drink." I handed one of my two bottles of beer to Kristoff.

"Only one. I've got to be up at three in the morning for site prep." With a sigh, he clinked his bottle against mine. It was his turn to be our scout. He was due to go ahead of us to our Inverness location, mapping out the site ready for the convoy to arrive later tomorrow morning.

Of course, I'd known about this for a while now, and I was taking full advantage. Guilt didn't even feature on my radar, not when so much was at stake.

All too soon, his eyelids began to droop. He'd fucking kill me when he found out what I'd done, but I was already resigned to my fate, and I'd made my peace with it. Ollie was what mattered. Nothing else.

"Want some help getting back to your cabin?"

He blinked up at me through bleary eyes. He'd arranged to stay in one of the A-frame cabins tonight, rather than the shared motorhome he normally slept in, and I was taking full advantage. "Please." He squinted at the bottle. "I must have had more than I thought."

I chuckled. "It happens all too easily. Come on." Wrapping my arm around his waist, I pulled him to his feet, taking a large percentage of his heavy body weight as we made our way past the long cabin where the feast was set out, and up the dirt road to the cluster of cabins. When we reached Kristoff's temporary accommodation, I opened the door with one hand—locks were rarely used here—and brought him inside, flicking on a small lamp that was positioned in the corner of the open space.

Helping him onto the bed, I waited a moment while he closed his eyes, muttering something about taking his clothes off and setting an alarm. But the drug was quick-acting, and all too soon his words turned to soft, even breaths, his features relaxed in sleep.

Easing my hand into his pocket, I liberated him from his car keys. Now it was time for the second part of my plan. Closing the cabin door behind me, I headed down to my motorhome, which had been driven here by one of the other cirque members. Inside, I prised open the secret compartment beneath the sink and pulled out a bundle of notes. A strange feeling stole over me as I placed the notes in the bottom of Ollie's bag and then carefully packed his belongings on top. I rubbed my hand across my pecs. My chest hurt. I felt...sad. A sadness that I'd never experienced before.

It reinforced my belief that I was doing the right thing.

After stowing Ollie's bag in Kristoff's SUV, I headed back to join the feast. By now, most of the cirque members had imbibed the alcohol that was freely on offer, and there was a relaxed, joyous atmosphere. My gaze was immediately drawn to Ollie, standing off to the side with a plate of food he was picking at, all alone and so fucking beautiful that it took all of my willpower to act casual and stay where I was, rather than stride across the room and take him in my arms.

Instead, as much as it pained me to do so, I made a point of conversing with others, gradually drawing closer to my boy. By the time I reached him, the feast was almost over, and Ollie was becoming visibly agitated. It hadn't escaped my notice that he'd made himself absent every time we'd dealt with one of the Chosen, and I was certain that tonight would be no exception. I wished that he'd embrace our lifestyle, but I knew there was a strong possibility that he'd never be okay with what we did. That was one of the reasons I'd put my plan into place tonight. The only thing that mattered to me was that my boy was safe and had a chance at happiness. He hadn't had much of that in his life thus far, and I'd do whatever I could to give it to him, even though it meant certain death for me.

Oliver was worth everything.

I'd reached Ollie before the Chosen were revealed, but as I'd expected, he was ready to leave, slipping away into the night like a shadow. Before he could disappear, I pulled him aside, pressing Kristoff's keys into his palm and curling his fingers around them.

"Wait in the SUV for me. I'll come for you."

His eyes shot to mine, full of questions, but I gave a slight shake of my head. Now wasn't the time. He'd find out soon enough.

After the killing was over and the crowd had begun to disperse, I waited behind until everyone had finally left. Only then did I make my way towards the SUV, keeping an eye and ear out for anyone who might see me. For once, I felt no arousal from the events of the evening, my mind too focused on what was to come, so much so that I barely paid attention to the screams of the Chosen, nor the delicious lifeblood that drained from their bodies. I made it safely to the car and slid inside, thankful for the tinted windows that hid me from view. Ollie was curled up on the seat next to me, fast asleep, the waves of his hair falling across his forehead and his lashes dusting his cheeks, and the pain in my chest that I'd felt earlier returned with a vengeance. I'd never get to see him like this again.

Thinking of what was to come hurt too much. I still had a few hours to wait until I could put the next part of my plan into place, so I set an alarm and let my eyes fall closed.

All too soon, the soft beep of the alarm sounded, and I blinked awake. The complex was dark and silent around us, the outside lights switched off to conserve energy, although I knew there were strategically placed motion sensor lights that would activate when I drove away. But if everything went to plan, no one would think twice. Everyone knew that Kristoff was due to drive ahead in the early hours of the morning to mark out our next site, and his SUV leaving the complex shouldn't trigger any alerts. My jaw set, I clenched my fist around the steering wheel with one hand and started up the engine with the other.

The soft purr of the car was magnified in the absolute silence, and I wasted no time in swinging out of the parking space, bumping down the road to the gates. They swung open as I neared—on a sensor, designed to keep unwanted visitors out and to make it easy for those on the complex to leave. I still held my breath for what felt like forever, until we were on the road leading north, the complex swallowed up by the forest behind us.

I set the satnav for my pre-arranged destination, checking the time. We'd arrive ten minutes early, all being well, and then...

Fuck. I swallowed hard, my throat working as I clenched the steering wheel in an iron grip. It was going to be so hard to let go of my boy. The hardest thing I'd ever have to do.

Glancing over at Ollie, still peacefully asleep, I knew I was making the right decision. No matter what happened to me, I'd do it. For him.

24
OLLIE

When I awoke, I was no longer in the SUV. I was at the side of the road. The SUV was to my left, visible only because of the headlights pointing away from me, and on my right was blackness. I heard the sound of waves lapping at the shore, and it didn't take a genius to work out that I was on the coast.

How had I ended up here, and why?

Arms closed around me, and I immediately lashed out, before a soft voice murmured in my ear, "Hey. It's me."

I relaxed into Dima's embrace, my own arms closing around him. Stretching upwards, I angled my head to where I thought his mouth was, brushing my lips across his and feeling him sigh against me.

"Where are we?" I pressed a kiss to his jaw, his stubble rasping over my skin as I spoke.

"I need you to listen to me carefully, Ollie, and do exactly as I say. Here's your bag." He took my hand, closing it around the familiar straps. "In a few minutes, you'll see a light. There's a boat. It'll take you to the Shetland Islands. As soon as you arrive, you'll see another boat at the docks. It'll take you to Norway. In your bag there's identification—a passport and qualifications, as well as money. Everything you need to start a new life. You'll have a new name, but you'll be free. No one will be able to trace you. Even I don't know exactly where you're going, but I've made sure you'll end up somewhere you can make something of yourself."

My jaw dropped. "*What*?" I gasped. "How? Why?"

"Because you're not happy in the cirque. Every day, your spirit grows heavier. I won't let your light be extinguished, and I want you to have a chance at a happy life." He cupped my jaw, and I felt his breath on my cheek as he lowered his head to mine. "I can't bear the thought of you being sad, sweetheart. You mean too much to me." Lips pressed softly against the corner of my mouth. "You're going to succeed. You're going to live to an old age, and you're going to be happy."

When he stepped backwards, I reached for him, my mind reeling. Tears welled up in my eyes, and I could barely choke out the words. "D-don't leave me. Please."

"I have to," he whispered, and I caught the crack in his voice as he dived into the SUV and slammed the door shut behind him.

No.

I pounded on the door, yanking at the handle, but it wouldn't open.

The engine started up with a roar.

And then...then he left me.

Alone, in the darkness, at the side of a deserted road, my only company the sound of the waves and the stars blanketing the sky.

***

My phone had thrown up some interesting information. Using the torch feature, I'd discovered a bundle of money right at the bottom of my bag. I'd stopped counting after the first ten thousand euros, shocked at how much Dima had left me. In the weak light, I'd examined the ID. John Samuels, age twenty, dual British and Norwegian nationality. It was everything I needed to begin a new life, and the boat was coming for me, but I didn't want it. Not even a bit. If I left now, I'd be sentencing Dima to death. Judge had made it crystal clear that our lives were tied together, and if I were to disappear, Dima's life would be forfeit. Even if I had been tempted to take up the opportunity Dima had provided me with, that alone would be enough to make me stay.

But it wasn't just that.

He'd arranged all this for *me*.

Which meant...I must be more important to him than I'd realised. My heart was swelling, every single part of me straining towards the direction we'd come from. He'd made a clear statement, putting my wellbeing above his own, and I wouldn't let him pay for what he'd done.

It was time to use all my resources, and to get to him.

Before it was too late.

25

DIMA

My head bowed as I knelt in the centre of the ring. Judge stood before me, his face grim, and in the gallery, the faces of the company were solemn. No one had expected it would come to this. Yet if I were given the same choices again, I'd choose Ollie. Every single time.

"You understand the consequences of your actions."

"I do." I blew out a heavy breath, my fingers digging into my thighs. My only hope now was that my death would be quick and merciful. Ollie would be well on his way to his new life by now, and that thought kept me from losing it. My beautiful boy would find happiness, even though it would be without me.

"How could you throw your life away for some dick?" Teeth's arms were folded across his chest, disbelief all over his face as he stood next to Judge.

"He's not some dick," I ground out. "He means everything to me. You think I'd do this for nothing? I can get dick any time I want. The point is, Ollie's special. He deserves the whole fucking world, and you should know that after working with him."

Teeth snarled in reply, but Judge shot him a warning look, and he slunk away from the ring to sit in the gallery.

"Wait!" a commanding voice sounded from behind me, and Judge froze in place as Vivienne rushed into the ring. "Stop this. They're soulmates. You know this. Mercy spoke of this with you yesterday. She knew it the second she laid eyes on them together." She reached up to take Judge's face between her hands. "My love, please listen. You cannot take Dima's life."

Judge's gaze flicked from Vivienne to me, and then back again. His mouth turned down, and he shook his head sadly. "So you believe. If they're soulmates, where is the boy?"

A collective gasp came from the assembled company, and at the same time, two words rang out, loud and clear. "I'm here."

There was a roaring in my ears, and my heart pounded so hard I could have sworn it was about to punch through my ribcage. Launching myself upright, I spun around, a hoarse cry falling from my lips as I took in the sight before me. *Ollie*. Dusty, dishevelled, and vibrating with anger as he stalked towards us, but he was *here*. He'd come back.

Fuck. What did this mean?

"First of all." Ollie's jaw was set, and his words were spoken through gritted teeth as he held Judge's gaze with no fear. "You lay a hand on him, and I will fucking end you, even if I die doing it. You might be the one in charge, but don't even think about underestimating me." His gaze flew to mine. "Second of all, *Dima*—" He spat my name. "—don't you fucking dare assume what's best for me again. My life is here, with the man I love, and even though I know the others haven't accepted me yet, I'm prepared to work until they do. You left me alone, in the dark, and I know you thought you were doing the right thing, but there's no way I'm letting you go until you decide you've had enough of me."

"Ollie. H-how?" It was the only question my brain could come up with, my mind completely overwhelmed with the fact that he was here, he'd gone up against Judge, and...and he'd said *the man I love*.

He stepped into the ring, his honey eyes filled with fire. "I walked until my torch gave out, which was the same time as my phone ran out of battery. Then I walked some more, following the road. When it started getting light, I happened to get lucky by flagging down a lorry that was travelling south, and the driver dropped me about a mile from here." His harsh gaze softened as he stopped right in front of me. "But I would have walked the whole fucking way if I had to. I understand why you did what you did, but you need to understand that I'd never let you give up everything for me."

"Ollie." My legs gave out and I dropped to my knees. "You...you mean everything to me."

The final traces of anger disappeared from his face as he stared down at me in wonder. "I don't know how..."

Trailing off, he shook his head. Then he lowered himself to his knees, shifting forwards so he could press his forehead against mine. "I love you, Dima."

I was helpless. Nothing on earth could have prepared me for the way my soul fucking sang at his words. "Ollie. My Ollie." I pulled him into my arms. "I didn't know what love was until you came along. If you're here to stay, I promise I'll never let you go again."

"I'm here to stay," he whispered. "I'm yours for as long as you'll have me."

Smiling, I brushed a soft kiss against his lips. "You're mine, sweet boy. My only one. How does that sound?"

"That sounds like I'm dreaming, but I want it to be true." Drawing back, he held my gaze, his eyes shining. "You'll probably have to convince me that all of this is real. Because you're you—" He waved his hand up and down. "—and I'm me."

"Enough. You're fucking perfect for me." I pressed a hard kiss against his lips. "I don't want anyone else. I choose you. Only you."

Ollie's gaze searched mine, a slow smile curving over his full lips. Climbing to his feet, he turned to face Judge. "If you'll allow me back and I'm here to stay, I'd like to change something."

Judge raised a brow. "Do you believe you're in a position to make demands?"

"No." Ollie shook his head. "But I hope you'll see reason. I hitchhiked over a hundred miles to get here, so I hope you can understand how serious I am about being here." Shooting me a sideways glance, he added, "With Dima."

Vivienne gave a pointed cough, and Judge sighed, throwing out his hands. "Go ahead."

I noticed Florin and Darius sneaking into the big top, taking seats in the gallery close to Teeth. Darius looked as if he was barely holding himself back from rushing into the ring, agitation clear in his eyes, and something inside me warmed at the thought that my friend would likely have done something both brave and inadvisable, should my life still be on the line.

As I stood, Ollie slid his fingers between mine. His hand was trembling, and I marvelled all over again at his courage. The fact that he was here, and he was stating his case, knowing Judge was well within his rights to end us both if he felt we deserved it. "Okay. I hate being stuck in the dark in the fortune teller tent. It's...it makes me feel so alone. I was used to being alone all my life, but I don't want that anymore. I want to be a part of this community. Properly."

"What about the Chosen?"

Everyone turned to look at Darius, who was studying Ollie carefully. Murmurs of agreement came from the assembled crowd.

Ollie's shoulders stiffened, and then he shook his head again. "You're right. I need...I need to face up to the parts of the cirque I've been struggling with." His gaze slid to Teeth. "That begins with you."

"Me? What does that mean?" Teeth seemed unsure

for once in his life, and I couldn't have stopped my grin if I'd tried.

"It means that I know you don't respect me, and that needs to change." Ollie beckoned him forwards. "I had a lot of time to think on my journey back here, and I know what needs to be done. Fight me. Let's have it out, right here, right now."

It took all the self-control I had to remain silent, but I knew if I interfered, I'd make everything worse.

"Very well," Teeth ground out. "But it must be a fair fight. No interference from anyone." He shot me a pointed look.

"So be it." Judge's voice raised. "The boy has returned to us. He says he's prepared to embrace the Cirque des Masques fully, and if he does so, you are to accept him as your own. As a brother. We are here to bear witness to this fight. When it is over, we will continue as planned. After tonight's show, Oliver will partake in our ritual, and prove that he belongs with us."

He cracked his whip, the sound echoing through the big top.

"You may begin."

The ring emptied out, until only me, Dima, and Teeth remained. Dima leaned down to me, speaking too low for anyone else to hear. "I don't care what the rules are. If Teeth hurts you, I'll make him pay."

"This is my fight. Trust me to do this," I whispered, squeezing his hand. He inclined his head, accepting my words, and then left the ring. I knew if it came down to it, he wouldn't hesitate to step in, but I knew he realised this was something I needed to do. Calling on all of the skills I'd picked up from my years on the streets, I began to circle Teeth. The clown was bigger than me, his teeth could rip my flesh to shreds, and his talons could do serious damage.

But I had a few tricks up my own sleeve. Literally.

Finding Florin and Darius when I'd entered the site had been a stroke of luck. They'd both been so relieved to see me, urging me to get to the big top to stop Judge from ending Dima's life, Florin hadn't even noticed when I'd liberated him from one of his knives. I palmed the one I had in my grip, my hand hidden beneath the sleeve of my hoodie, and continued to circle Teeth slowly, waiting for the moment he'd inevitably rush at me.

In my pocket was a small length of rope, which I'd knotted, ready for this. As I'd told Teeth, I'd had a lot of time to think on the journey here. The lorry driver who had given me a lift was more than happy to talk without expecting a reply, and it had given me a chance to plan. I knew what I needed to do. My plan was a simple one, and I just needed a bit of luck on my side. I didn't want to draw this fight out either—it wasn't about the fight itself. It was about showing him that he shouldn't underestimate me, that I could hold my own against him.

"Come on then. Show me those sharp teeth and claws," I taunted, and Teeth snarled at me, his eyes glittering with malice. He rushed me, as I'd expected, and I twisted my body out of the way, spinning around behind him and flicking the knife out, slicing into the meat of his bicep to draw the first blood. With a howl, he spun around, his fingers slashing through the air, one of his talons scraping down the side of my face. The sting was instant, but I ignored it. We'd both drawn blood, and I needed him to think he had the upper hand. When he lunged at me again, I ducked enough to avoid his teeth and claws, but let his body clash with mine, sending me stumbling forwards.

He grinned, his pointed teeth glinting under the

spotlight, and I smiled to myself. Time to end this. This time when he came at me, I slid down and around, sweeping out my leg and sending him crashing to the floor, face down. His arms instinctively came out to brace his fall, but I was already leaping onto his back with the knotted rope in my hands. I yanked his arms behind him, twisting the rope around his wrists and pulling it tight, and then drew the knife from my sleeve and pressed the point into the back of his neck. "Did you know," I said, pressing a little harder, "that I could sever your spinal cord, right here, right now? You'd be instantly dead."

Teeth bucked upwards, trying to dislodge my grip, spitting dirt from his mouth as he swore at me. I hung on, lowering my head to his ear.

"Don't fucking underestimate me again. You respect me, and I'll respect you." I rolled off him, and he managed to climb to his feet, his hands still bound behind his back. His eyes met mine, and his mouth curled into a snarl. He spat at my feet, and then turned on his heel and stalked away.

"Ollie!" Florin bounded into the ring, throwing his arms around me as soon as I was standing again. A bright grin stretched across his face. "You stole my knife again!"

"Yeah. Here." After wiping the blade clean with the sleeve of my hoodie, I handed it back to him.

Bouncing on the balls of his feet, he clapped his hands together, his eyes widening. "I've had the best idea! You can be in my act. What do you say? We get to play with knives. It'll be so much fun."

Be in Florin's act? In the ring, under the spotlight? Throwing knives, maybe incorporating my pickpocketing skills into the routine? I smiled at him. "If Judge agrees, then yes. I'll be in your act."

"Leave it to me. I'll sort out all the details. We can practice this afternoon, ready for tonight's show." He darted away, straight towards Judge.

"Everybody, out." Dima's command cut through the low murmurs of those gathered, and I turned to him. His eyes were dark and heated, and I knew that look. Fuck. I took a deep breath, my cock rapidly lengthening as I took in the way he was dragging his gaze over my body. "Ollie stays. The rest of you, go."

27

DIMA

Everyone dispersed at the crack of Judge's whip. Before he left, he bowed his head to me, a hint of a smile lifting his lips. Then he was gone, and I strode into the centre of the empty ring where Ollie waited for me, his eyes burning with desire. I wanted him. More than I'd ever wanted anyone or anything. The way he'd just taken Teeth down...my cock was rock hard and fucking dripping from the little display he'd put on, and the sight of that scarlet trail of blood down his cheek...it was so erotic, and I had to have him, right now.

"On your knees," I rasped when I reached him, and he immediately dropped down, a soft moan falling from his throat as I sank my fingers into his hair. "See what you do to me?" I tugged his head forwards, his nose sliding along the side of my thick erection. "You make me so fucking hard."

His eyes lifted to mine, his pupils blown as he stared up at me. "You do the same to me."

"Take me out. I need your mouth on my cock. Then I'm going to take you back home, get you cleaned up, and fill you with my cum."

He shuddered against me, undoing my trousers with trembling fingers. I could see his cock tenting his trousers, and my mouth watered. I wanted a taste of him.

But then his mouth closed around the head of my cock, his tongue dragging across my slit, tasting my precum, and my vision whited out. I thrust forwards, slamming my length into him, and fucked his face hard and fast, holding his head in place. He swallowed around me, his fingers pressing against my perineum while tears ran down his face, and my release hit me like a freight train.

"Fuck. Ollie." My legs shook, and I wasn't sure how I managed to remain upright. He gasped for breath as I drew him off me, swallowing again, his face a beautiful mess with the tears running down his cheeks, the scarlet smear of blood, and my cum at the corners of his mouth.

"Dima." His voice had gone hoarse from the way I'd fucked his throat. Licking his lips, he blinked up at me. "Dima."

"Come here." I pulled him to his feet, wrapping my arms around him and holding him to me until I could breathe properly again. I was aware of his hardness between us, and I'd take care of that in a moment. But first...I lifted his chin, and kissed the tears from his face, and then pressed soft kisses along the cut on his cheek. He moaned, arching into me, trying to get some friction on his neglected cock. Brushing a kiss against his plush lips, I stroked my hand through his soft hair. "My beautiful boy. Do you trust me?"

"Yes."

"Wait here." I let him go, tugging my trousers back up and then striding over to the side of the ring. Picking up one of my fire whips, I examined the length of it. I was no Judge, but I excelled at my fire routine, and although I hadn't performed this particular act in a long time—and never in a sexual way—I trusted my own abilities.

After clipping a second, much smaller whip to my belt, I gathered up the fire whip. Returning to the centre of the ring, I instructed Ollie to clasp his hands behind his back. "I need you to stand completely still. Can you do that for me?"

He nodded, slightly dazed, his pupils huge and dark as he stared at me. I trusted him not to flinch, not after the way he'd remained cool and collected when Florin had thrown those knives at him.

Counting my paces, I stepped away from him until I judged I was the correct distance away. Ollie was a statue before me, gazing at me with complete trust.

I lifted my hand, twisting it, sending the whip flying out in front of me in a curling movement, and then cracked it again. It wrapped around Ollie's body, and then I tugged. He stumbled forwards, and I tugged again, bringing him closer to me as I circled around him. When I reached him, he was breathing hard, bound and at my mercy. There was a damp patch on the front of his trousers, his cock an obscene line that made my mouth water, and I knew he was on a hair trigger, ready to come at my command.

Coming to a stop behind him, I lowered my mouth to his ear. "You like this? Do you like being helpless? I could do whatever I wanted with you, couldn't I?"

He moaned, his head falling back against my shoulder. Kissing down the side of his throat, I reached around and stroked one finger down his torso, tracing the lines of the whip that held him bound. When I reached the waistband of his trousers, I paused, and he whined, thrusting forwards desperately.

I fingered the small whip at my waist, and a slow smile spread across my face. Lowering his trousers and underwear carefully, avoiding any friction on his erect cock, I dragged my teeth back up his throat to his ear, where I lightly bit down.

"D-Dima." His voice was thick, slurred. "Please."

"Look at you, fucking dripping for me." I palmed the whip, my own cock lengthening at the sight. "Do you want to come?"

"Please. *Please*."

Lifting my hand, I traced the very end of the small whip gently across the exposed head of his cock. It was the barest touch, but he gasped, arching upwards. "Oh, fuck. *Dima*."

I slid the whip back across his skin, precum glistening on the leather as I slowly drew it over his dripping cock. A moan fell from his throat, and I knew that one more touch would send him over the edge.

"Come for me, Ollie." Dropping the whip, I wrapped

my hand around his throbbing length, and that was all it took. His cock pulsed in my grip and his body shook against me, his cum painting the floor of the ring.

Fuuuuck. I needed to be inside him. Now.

"Let's go home."

Back at the motorhome, we stripped down and entered the shower, our hands all over each other, both of us hard and desperate. When our bodies were cleansed, I picked up Ollie, carrying him to our bedroom and lowering him onto our bed. The need to be inside him was almost too much to bear, but I wanted him to have the choice.

"If you want to fuck me, you can."

He shook his head as his body arched up against mine. "No. Maybe one day. But I want you to fill me with your cum like you promised. Then tonight when you see me doing my new act in the ring, you can remember what we did. Know that your cum's dripping out of me."

"Fucking hell," I groaned, fisting my cock. "Turn over and spread your legs. I need to be inside you now."

I lowered my head, working my tongue over his rim until he was shuddering on the bed, pushing back against me. I lubed up and opened him up with my fingers, brushing over his prostate, his whimpers and moans making my cock throb, desperate to be inside the tight heat of his hole.

"Now. Please," he gasped, arching back, raising his

gorgeous ass as he came up onto his knees, and I lined myself up, pressing a kiss to his shoulder.

"You beg so fucking sweetly."

Then I thrust all the way home, both of us groaning as I filled him with my thick length. He ground down into the bed as I snapped my hips forwards, his breath catching in his throat. "Dima. Fuck me hard."

I couldn't hold back, pounding him hard and fast, my hand snaking underneath his body to his cock. Wrapping my fingers around his shaft, I stroked up and down in time with my thrusts, both of us hurtling towards the edge. We exploded almost together, the first pulses of his orgasm triggering mine, and I stroked him through his release as I did what I'd promised and filled him with my cum.

When it was over, I pulled him into my arms. "That was incredible. You're incredible. You mean everything to me, Ollie."

He smiled against my skin. "You mean everything to me, too."

28

OLLIE

The spotlight was shining, the spectators mere shadows around the brightness of the ring. From behind the curtain, I watched as Dima entranced the crowd, fire swirling around him. He was mesmerising and so fucking sexy that I had to actively work to avoid my arousal from becoming too obvious. It would be my turn soon. My first time in the ring. Florin had devised a simple routine that we'd expand on when we had more time, and I couldn't wait to put my skills to use in front of an audience.

"Oliver." I twisted around to see Judge, clad in his full ringmaster outfit and mask, dark and forbidding. He stretched out his hand to me. "This is for you to wear tonight, as is tradition."

I took the object from him, moving closer to the light so I could examine it. It was a mask made of faded black silk with ornate gold detailing, the stitching tarnished with age. My gaze shot to his, my mouth falling open. "What's this?"

Through the holes in his mask, his eyes gleamed. "I assume Dima has told you of the cirque's history. Legend says that this mask once belonged to the boy whose heart was stolen, back when the cirque first began. The girl had it made posthumously in his honour." Stepping closer, he lowered his voice. "None of us know for sure, of course, but what we do know is that it's extremely old, and one of our most precious artifacts."

I swallowed hard. "And you want *me* to wear it? Are you sure?"

"Yes. All our performers wear it for their inaugural time in the ring. Therefore, you will also wear this. You're one of us, after all."

"I am?"

He chuckled softly. "You and I both know that this is where you were always meant to be. Vivienne saw it from the beginning, and while I may have had my reservations at first, your actions today have proven your true intentions to me. Some of the others may still need convincing, but I trust you'll take care of that after the show."

After the show. The Chosen. Licking my suddenly dry lips, I nodded. I'd do whatever it took to ensure that everyone knew I was committed to the cirque. I was all in. "I will."

"Good." He squeezed my shoulder. "I look forward to your act."

When he swept away with a dramatic swirl of his

cloak, I unfastened my mask, replacing it with the new one. It felt soft and light against my skin, settling over the contours of my face like it was made for me.

"Pretty," a voice whispered in my ear. "Ready to play with knives?"

I grinned at Florin. "Yeah. I'm ready."

Dima came striding out of the ring, and I heard the crowds gasp behind him as Vivienne swung high on the trapeze with two of the other performers. He came to a stop right in front of me, his chest heaving and his torso glistening with sweat. "Break a leg," he murmured, dipping down to kiss me. "I'll be here watching you."

The tentmen rolled Florin's wheel past us, entering the ring, and I leaned forwards to press another kiss to Dima's addictive mouth before I followed them in. When I turned away, he caught me around the wrist, stopping my movements.

"Ollie."

"Yeah?"

He looked down at me, his lips curving into a smile as his thumb stroked across my pulse point. "I love you."

My heart exploded out of my chest, my own smile spreading across my face. "I love you, too."

"I know. Now, go out there and prove to everyone just how much you belong with us, and I'll be right here waiting for you when it's all over."

I nodded, and he released me.

Then I stepped into the spotlight.

It felt like the act flew by in the blink of an eye. Just as we'd practiced earlier, I "stole" Florin's knives, swinging onto the back of one of the performer's motorbikes, circling the ring and whipping the crowd into a frenzy. Holding on to the motorbike securely with one hand, I threw the knives at the empty spinning wheel one by one, before allowing Florin's "henchmen" to capture me, dragging me from the motorbike when it slowed at the pre-planned moment. After putting on a show of me struggling, they dragged me towards the wheel where Florin was retrieving his knives. When the henchmen had tied me to the wheel, they set it spinning, and my little psycho friend laughed and launched the knives at me with fast, deadly accuracy.

The spectators went crazy, and a wide grin overtook my face.

The high of the performance was like nothing else.

This was it. This was where I belonged. Right here, in the Cirque des Masques.

29

OLLIE

Clad in my original mask once again, I made my way to the clearing to await the Chosen. My palms were clammy, and my heart rate was through the roof, but I knew this was the final test I needed to pass. I needed to prove that I wasn't going to run, that I could see it through to the very end.

The clearing that had been marked out in the ground earlier tonight was empty, members of the cirque around the edges, forming a circle with a gap for the Chosen to pass through. Not everyone was in attendance, but the majority had turned up, most likely to see if I would follow through this time.

I came to a stop next to Dima, and he placed a hand on my lower back, speaking softly into my ear. "All you need to do is embrace the curse. Do that, and it'll all become easy."

Embrace the curse. The curse of bloodlust and a crazed need for sex...was that what I wanted? Or would it be enough to steel myself to watch what happened tonight, to stand my ground until it was all over?

Flames flickered and logs crackled from the bonfire behind the clearing. One of the dogs whined, restless, while the other cocked its head, listening. The assembled company was silent, clad in black, all masked.

Someone jostled me, and I swung around to see Teeth, his mouth bared in the rictus grin that I just knew he spent hours practicing in the mirror maze. I rolled my eyes, and his grin softened, turning genuine.

My brows flew to the top of my head when he held out a hand to me. "You have my respect."

It took a minute for his words to register, they were so unexpected. When I managed to gather myself, I held out my own hand, shaking his briefly. "And you have mine."

He inclined his head, before disappearing as quickly as he'd arrived, taking his place over on the opposite side of the clearing. I looked up at Dima to find him watching me with a small smile. "That was unexpected."

"Perhaps not." His thumb rubbed across the small of my back. "I'm proud of you."

"Thanks," I said quietly. We fell silent again as we waited for the Chosen to arrive. Florin slipped into place across from me, between Teeth and Darius, his usual bright, excited smile on his face as he flipped one of his knives from one hand to the other. Darius pressed a kiss to the side of his head, tugging Florin into him.

The sense of anticipation grew until the night air was almost vibrating with it.

When the bound, gagged figure was dragged into the clearing and thrown to their knees on the dirty ground, I got my first good look at tonight's Chosen. Judge read out a list of crimes that made me sick to my stomach. The man, in his sixties, had swindled a huge number of unsuspecting elderly people out of their life savings, leaving them with nothing, and then he'd set fire to his own home with his wife trapped inside, planning to claim both the house insurance and her life insurance. As the house caught fire, he'd driven to the pub where he'd celebrated with pint after pint. He'd driven away, drunk, and mowed two people down, a fifteen-year-old boy and his mother. Both had later died in hospital.

Somehow, even after all that, he'd managed to get away. He'd grown bold, splashing the cash, spending huge sums on horse racing, until there came a point where it had almost all dwindled away. That was when he'd become desperate, too addicted to his new lifestyle, and he'd planned a robbery of a small, local shop. The robbery hadn't gone to plan, and although the man escaped again, he fatally stabbed the shop owner, leaving him to bleed out on the floor as he made his escape.

That wasn't the only thing that had happened that night, though. Driving erratically, he spun across the road and crashed into a car coming in the opposite direction, and although he once again escaped, the driver of the other car wasn't so lucky. By the time ambulances arrived on the scene, it was too late.

I closed my eyes, breathing in and out deeply as

Judge's words washed over me. Pictures played across my mind. All those lives, ruined or gone, and this man had escaped every single time.

Embrace the curse.

My eyes opened, and my gaze fixed on him. Straightening my shoulders, I removed my mask and then stepped into the circle.

Tonight, the man's luck had run out. Tonight, he was our Chosen, and justice would be served.

I knew what to do.

The rest of the company removed their masks, remaining silent and still, waiting for me to act. Flicking my gaze to Florin, I held out my hand, and Florin darted over to me, placing the knife in my palm. *Join our murder circus*, he mouthed, and I gave him a savage grin in return.

My fingers curved around the knife's handle as I began to circle the man. His eyes were bulging as he stared up at me, his throat working as he tried to speak from behind the gag, tears and drool running down his face and over his chin.

Embrace the curse.

"You're here to face the consequences of your actions," I said. "You took without thought, without remorse. And now you're going to pay." With that, I launched forwards, stabbing the knife into his side and twisting it. He screamed from behind the gag, and Judge cracked his whip. One of the dogs prowled into the clearing, teeth bared in a snarl. Another crack from Judge's whip, and the dog leapt, sinking its teeth into the man's arm. As I straightened up, Florin barrelled into the circle, his face alight, and slashed the knife across the side of the man's throat. The spray of blood landed on both of our faces, and when he glanced up at me, I felt it for the first time. The bloodlust, fizzing through my veins.

Fuck. It was *euphoric.*

Spinning to Dima, I took in the way he was palming the huge bulge between his legs as he stared at me with lust in his eyes, and my cock jumped, hardening so fast I was almost dizzy with it.

This was it. First the bloodlust, then the sexual need.

I understood. I embraced it.

Everything clicked into place, and I *knew.*

I'd been afflicted, and now I was truly one of the cirque.

Dima pulled me to him, his mouth coming down on mine. "I understand now," I murmured against his lips when we broke apart, angling my hips forwards, his thigh a delicious friction against my cock. Fuck. He felt so good.

His eyes met mine, and pride shone in them. "I never had any doubt. Go and finish what you started, and then we can celebrate, just you and me." His hand traced across the spray of blood on my face. "Fuck, Ollie. I need to make you mine so fucking badly."

"Dima. I'm yours. Always." Our mouths met again in a hard kiss, before I tore myself away to return to my task, buzzing with this new euphoria that was filling every part of my being. It was a high I never wanted to come down from.

As I rejoined Florin and, together, we ended a life with our own version of justice, I smiled.

I had a home. A man who loved me. A family, a little fucked up and twisted, but loyal to the end.

For the first time in my life, I finally had a place where I belonged.

WELCOME TO THE SHOW...

S o this is where our story ends. As with most legends, there is indeed a grain of truth to the rumours.

For those unlucky enough to see the faces behind the masks...well, they aren't cursed for all eternity. But those faces will be the last they ever see.

If you are one of the lucky ones to visit the cirque as a spectator, however, prepare for a performance you will never forget. Take your seat in the stands and prepare to be amazed. Darkness will fall over the big top, anticipation in the air as you lean forwards, trying to make out anything in the shadows.

Then a spotlight will appear in the centre of the ring, and it will begin. Smoke will swirl in the air. The ringmaster's whip will crack, echoing around the tent, and then he will speak.

Welcome to the Cirque des Masques.

Enjoy the show.

THE END

Also by Becca Steele

LSU Series

(M/M college romance)

Collided

Blindsided

Sidelined

The Four Series

(M/F college suspense romance)

The Lies We Tell

The Secrets We Hide

The Havoc We Wreak

A Cavendish Christmas (free short story)*

The Fight In Us

The Bonds We Break

The Darkness In You

Alstone High Standalones

(new adult high school romance)

Trick Me Twice (M/F)

Cross the Line (M/M)

In a Week (free short story)* (M/F)

Savage Rivals (M/M)

London Players Series

(M/F rugby romance)

The Offer

London Suits Series

(M/F office romance)

The Deal

The Truce

The Wish (a festive short story) *

Other Standalones

Cirque des Masques (M/M dark circus romance)

Mayhem (M/F Four series dark spinoff) *

Heatwave (M/F summer short story) *

Boneyard Kings Series (with C. Lymari)

(RH/why-choose college suspense romance)

Merciless Kings

Vicious Queen

Ruthless Kingdom

Box Sets

Caiden & Winter trilogy (M/F)

(The Four series books 1-3)

all free short stories and bonus scenes are available from https://authorbeccasteele.com

**Key - M/F = Male/Female romance

M/M = Male/Male romance

RH = Reverse Harem/why-choose (one woman & 3+ men) romance

About the Author

Becca Steele is a USA Today and Wall Street Journal bestselling romance author. She currently lives in the south of England with a whole horde of characters that reside inside her head.

When she's not writing, you can find her reading or watching Netflix, usually with a glass of wine in hand. Failing that, she'll be online hunting for memes or making her 500th Spotify playlist.

Join Becca's Facebook reader group Becca's Book Bar, sign up to her mailing list, check out her Patreon, or find her via the following links:

facebook.com/authorbeccasteele

instagram.com/authorbeccasteele

bookbub.com/profile/becca-steele

goodreads.com/authorbeccasteele

patreon.com/authorbeccasteele

amazon.com/stores/Becca-Steele/author/B07WT6GWB2

Made in United States
Orlando, FL
03 July 2023